A Handful of Magic

Suddenly Henry seemed to buckle at the knees. He let out a gasp of horror and his eyes jerked fully open. And snatching desperately at the air he slowly tipped backwards into the werewolves' den.

Kit, son of the Queen's witch doctor, takes his best friend, Prince Henry, on a night time adventure to see the werewolves at the Tower of London. Henry falls into the den and is bitten, causing a rift between the Queen and Kit's father. The Queen sends for Stafford Sparks, the Royal Superintendent of Scientific Progress, to cure Henry, declaring that magic is dead and that electricity is the power of the future.

Kit is sent to live with his Aunt Pearl in her weird home on the tower of old St Paul's cathedral, but he is determined to save Henry from the clutches of Stafford Sparks and his electric shock treatment and prove that magic is still alive. But Kit's attempts to help his friend lead him into terrible danger in the tunnels under London, danger which even magic may not be able to overcome.

Stephen Elboz lives in Northamptonshire, and has had a variety of jobs, including being a dustman, a civil servant, and a volunteer on an archaeological dig. He now divides his time between teaching and writing. His first book, *The House of Rats*, won the Smarties Young Judges Prize for the 9–11 age category.

A Handful of Magic

Other books by Stephen Elboz

A Land Without Magic
The House of Rats
A Store of Secrets
The Tower at Moonville
Ghostlands
Temmi and the Flying Bears

A Handful of Magic

Stephen Elboz

OXFORD
UNIVERSITY PRESS

OXFORD
UNIVERSITY PRESS

Great Clarendon Street, Oxford OX2 6DP

Oxford University Press is a department of the University of Oxford.
It furthers the University's objective of excellence in research, scholarship,
and education by publishing worldwide in

Oxford New York

Auckland Bangkok Buenos Aires Cape Town Chennai
Dar es Salaam Delhi Hong Kong Istanbul Karachi Kolkata
Kuala Lumpur Madrid Melbourne Mexico City Mumbai Nairobi
São Paulo Shanghai Taipei Tokyo Warsaw

Oxford is a registered trade mark of Oxford University Press
in the UK and in certain other countries

First published 2000
Reprinted 2000
First published in this paperback edition 2001

British Library Cataloguing in Publication Data available

ISBN 0 19 275134 4

3 5 7 9 10 8 6 4

Typeset by AFS Image Setters Ltd, Glasgow
Printed in Great Britain by
Cox & Wyman Ltd, Reading, Berkshire

This book is for Hilary Miles and in
memory of our good friend Wendy Boswell,
who is very much missed.

And special thanks to Linda Hitchens who
was wizard at the computer keyboard
on my behalf.

Chapter One

I f Kit Stixby hadn't been so bored or hadn't been a wizard, he might have managed to keep himself out of trouble for once. But as he was both bored *and* a wizard, trouble was bound to follow. Sure enough on this particular day he had managed to turn every one of his father's silver spoons into frogs. Dozens of them—frogs of all shapes and sizes.

This, he told himself reasonably as he stood by the half empty cutlery drawer, was partly his father's fault: if his father hadn't owned so many spoons to begin with there would be far fewer frogs hopping around the big whitewashed kitchen. And not only hopping: they were in the dried fruits, had knocked over and broken several plates, and were squinting at their stretched faces reflected in the highly polished kettle.

Luckily Cook hadn't come in to start supper yet and it was Millie's afternoon off; Kit had practically the whole house to himself—and the frogs of course . . . ah yes, those frogs.

Kit yawned lazily. He supposed he'd better get on with the business of turning them back into something more at home beside a knife and fork rather than in the depths of a slimy pond. But when he next looked around he was surprised to find all the frogs had disappeared, each one somehow sensing what he meant to do.

Kit knew only *he* could make things vanish. The frogs were simply hiding. And as if to prove him right, at that moment he spotted the tea cosy trembling. Kit smiled to himself. Slowly and without a sound he crept up close, seized the cosy and flung it high into the air. Beneath it lurked a small, brilliantly yellow frog with hallmarks clearly visible on its top lip. Kit whooped excitedly as now—found out—the frog hopped desperately towards the only place of safety it knew—the cutlery drawer.

'Oh no you don't!' bawled Kit.

He pointed, the air fizzled with magic (like bacon frying) and the frog-spoon, caught in mid hop, landed with a metallic clatter and was still. Kit blew on his finger as though it were a smoking gun, yet his moment of glory was not long lasting. To be precise it ended when he caught sight of a smouldering piece of buckled metal that should have been a nice shiny scalloped-handled teaspoon.

'That's not right,' he muttered to the magic inside him. 'Oh well . . . ' He shrugged carelessly. He allowed himself a mistake or two . . .

Like his father, Kit was tall and dark, and his hair sprouted so thickly that neither comb nor magic seemed able to keep it under control (not that Kit minded—once magic had accidentally given him a set of green curls). His eyes were dark too, dark and sharp, and just then narrowing as they spotted another tiny movement.

This time he was too quick and rash, he pointed and released the full force of his magic. It sparked upon a copper pan, which giving an angry *D-ANG!* jumped off its hook and crashed down upon Cook's marble worktop. To avoid being stung by his own deflected magic, Kit hastily threw himself to the floor . . . just in time. Magic streaked over his head, struck an earthenware jar upon a shelf opposite and exploded it into a hundred pieces, sending a cloud of Cook's best flour swirling into the air.

Kit jumped back up laughing himself stupid and brushing his hands together in a job-well-done kind of way, as if that was how he meant his magic to go.

Kit was justly proud of his wizardly powers which he had had since the age of three, quite young compared to most other wizards and witches who were more likely to be seven before they received theirs. It happened at night when Kit was asleep—afterwards he recalled nothing but a strange dream about wild flames and bright flashing lights. Next morning, Nurse looked in upon him and squealed. Kit was circling high above his bed, snoozing contentedly and quite unaware of the great thing that had happened to him.

Like all other children of magic families, the event had been celebrated with a Coming of Magic party attended by witch-aunts and wizard-uncles and lots of jealous cousins who were twice Kit's age yet couldn't blow a spark; which is the high point of any Coming of Magic party—blowing on the unlit candles on a special cake and lighting them (only those without magic blow on candles to put the flames *out*). Also at the party had been many presents of chocolate wands and A-B-C spell books; but best of all was Grandpa Wishbane's present—a magic carpet of Kit's very own, which was upstairs, carefully rolled up beneath his bed.

But for all that, perhaps the getting of his powers so young was an unfortunate thing in Kit's case, for he was not such a good wizard as he believed. Not yet anyway. Even now some of his latest creations showed signs of weak or slipshod magic. Some had entirely spoon heads and lacking eyes blundered into things; others had long handles for tails that pulled them back to earth whenever they tried to hop; and still others were half faded away, while at various places around the kitchen there would be heard from time to time a soft *pop*, and then a frog would vanish and a piece of twisted metal appear, clattering down as if thrown by a ghostly hand.

But Kit never thought about his shortcomings,

especially in magic, and especially now as he caught the distinctive sound of Cook's sensible shoes coming down the stone steps outside, Cook grunting at the steps' steepness.

Taking a long, slow look around, Kit was amazed to see the kitchen was not *quite* as orderly as Cook liked it. Cook with her temper that could go off like a volcano . . .

'Best she don't catch me here,' muttered Kit in a rare moment of wisdom. And with that he stepped over a blue spotted frog and slipped away to the upper part of the house.

Here he knew well—after years of it being drummed into him—to pass on his way without a sound. On no account would his father, Dr Stixby, tolerate any disturbance once he had entered his study. He was an important man—no less than the personal witch doctor to Queen Victoria and her family—so often had important work to do or, as was the case this evening, he received visits from equally important people, high up wizards and witches and their like. Kit hated it when they came, discussing highbrow magic and enchantments; he felt shut out and ignored. Secretly he did feel proud of his father and bragged about him often enough, yet he was careful not to show his father how much he admired him—Kit was too much in awe of him for that.

Dr Stixby's caller on this particular occasion was that funny little herbalist, Herbert Obb. Kit wrinkled up his nose at the thought of Mr Obb's restless watery eyes and nervous stammer, but especially as he remembered the smell of newly dug earth that always hung around him— the *worm smell* Kit called it. Mr Obb was a regular visitor at 24 Angel Terrace, and together he and Dr Stixby spent hours discussing new plants and their healing powers, and chopping up leaves and grinding roots, boiling everything down until the whole house reeked of rotting cabbages.

Kit in the hallway lingered by the umbrella stand, where it was easy to spot Mr Obb's broomstick amongst the others because it had pieces of dry moss in its twigs. The man actually used it for sweeping up! The thought horrified Kit and made him feel superior at the same time; he wondered whether to show his disapproval by leaving a delayed stink-bomb spell in Mr Obb's coat pocket. As he stood deciding he heard Dr Stixby's voice above the steady tick of the hallway's ancient grandfather clock.

'Of course I do find it all rather alarming.'

'In-in-in-indeed,' stammered Mr Obb.

Kit pulled a face but then his father continued.

'You know what I sometimes believe, Herbert? Sometimes I believe there will be no place left for magic in the future—and I'm not speaking of the far distant future either. In our own lifetime we shall be pushed aside by progress and there is nothing any of us can do about it.'

'Surely n-n-not. There must always be a n-n-need for magic.'

Kit paused, head tilted towards the solid mahogany door. Now this sounded more interesting, at least more interesting than cutting up bits of boring old plants. Without believing he was doing the slightest thing wrong, Kit crouched down on the colourful polished tiles and pressed his eye to the brass keyhole. Mr Obb and Dr Stixby sat facing each other in identical green leather chairs with a fire blazing between them; overhead a pair of glow-balls hovered, very dim, but reflecting in the mantel mirror. The rest of the room was darkly panelled and shadowy. Turning back to the two men, Kit noticed that each of them held a brandy glass which glinted in the firelight, along with Mr Obb's ridiculously large spectacles. This was unusual, thought Kit, his father never drank in the early evening in case there was need of him and he had to fly to the Palace.

Dr Stixby took a thoughtful sip and turned to gaze at the fire. He was elegantly dressed in a fine tailored suit; indeed the only outward sign he ever gave that he was a witch doctor and not, say, a banker or lawyer, was the bright emerald-green top hat he wore whenever he went out. Next to him, Kit saw with satisfaction, Mr Obb looked small and dreary, his pockets bulging with odds and ends, typical of any gardener; and both his collar and cuffs were badly frayed.

'H-h-has the Queen m-mentioned any-anything in par-par-particular to you?' enquired Mr Obb taking a nervous gulp of brandy.

Dr Stixby continued to stare deep into the leaping flames. 'She hasn't needed to, I simply get a strong sense of how things are and will be. The trouble with these times, Herbert, is that everyone demands what is new and exciting. Magic is viewed as creaky and old-fashioned—why have a few blessed with special powers when there is electricity, gas, and steam for everyone? I can't help worrying that magic is becoming more and more a thing of our grandparents' day—along with wind-power and clockwork.'

'T-tick-t-tock,' obliged Mr Obb with a nervous giggle.

Suddenly Dr Stixby turned his powerful, dark eyes on him, making poor Mr Obb jerk back into his chair as if hoping its arms might throw themselves around him for protection. 'And there is one man I blame above all others for the decline of witchcraft in the land today,' said Dr Stixby in a low growl.

Mr Obb nodded his head seeming to know already, but Dr Stixby reminded him all the same. 'Stafford Sparks—the Royal Superintendent of Scientific Progress—sitting like a little king at his Temple of Science up in Kensington.'

'O-o-o-oh yes. T-terrible man,' agreed Mr Obb wholeheartedly.

'And the Queen will have nothing said against him whatever he does: and what he does best is flatter her and keep her amused. Honestly, Herbert, you have never seen such an odd sight as the Queen cooing with pleasure at every new mechanical toy or gadget he sets before her, making it perform like a dog in a side-show, most of the time doing what any half decent wizard can do by magic in the first place. And folk have the gall to blame us wizards for bewitching and misleading people—ha!' Dr Stixby shook his head in sad disbelief. 'Stafford Sparks would drive magic and those who practise it into the sea if given half the chance.'

Mr Obb drank again. 'Thankfully, Ch-Ch-Charles, he h-h-hasn't the means t-t-to do it.'

'For the time being,' said Dr Stixby darkly.

At the keyhole on the far side of the door, Kit decided he was growing bored by so much solemn talk; it was like listening to one of Reverend Bland's unending Sunday sermons. He pointed to a patch of air and mumbled magic at it. A glow-ball filled the empty space, its centre brilliant white, its edges melting to buttercup yellow.

'Race you,' challenged Kit, and laughing wildly and forgetting to be quiet he thundered up the hallway stairs closely followed by his glow-ball, a comet-like tail stretching behind in its wake. At the top of the second flight, the race proceeded along a landing of crusty old wizard portraits, Kit only two beards ahead of his magic if measured against them. He burst through his door and threw himself laughing onto an unmade bed. Over him, the glow-ball (now without its tail) bobbed playfully, dripping its butter-melting light upon the cast-aside clothes and spell books, and the unreturned plates of mouldy crusts and shrivelled apple cores. Absolutely no one was allowed to enter Kit's room without first gaining his permission; and he had made sure it was completely

7

servant-proof by magically moving the door handle and lock, and making them invisible to their eyes. This explained why dust lay thick on all the furniture, and why amongst it there wasn't a single properly closed door or drawer.

Suddenly Kit stopped laughing and sat upright, listening. A small scratching sound came from his window. Outside it was already dark—a gloomy November evening with gas lamps glowing through bare trees. Kit nodded curtly and the glow-ball obeyed, crossing the room to the window.

By its light Kit saw something pressed up against the glass—scratching with its claw to be allowed in.

It was a tiny bat.

Chapter Two

'Hector!'

Kit let out a whoop of savage joy then bounded across to the window, threw it open and reached out into the cold, drab night to scoop up the little creature, feeling his tiny body shivering beneath soft damp fur. Safe in his cupped hands, Kit carried him back to his bed and sat down.

He tickled the bat's belly. 'Well, little fellow, I haven't seen you for quite a while,' he cooed affectionately.

Hector, from South America, was a pet bat once owned by Kit, but he had given him to his best friend, Henry, on the understanding that, 'Hector can fly secret messages between us—at night when no one else can see.' Secrecy was important because not only was Henry Kit's best friend, he was also Queen Victoria's youngest and favourite grandchild, who had been raised by the Queen at the Palace since his father died and his mother became unable to cope. The two boys had much in common—not least one distant parent each.

Since birth, Henry had never been a particularly strong or healthy boy, and the Royal Witch Doctor had been summoned frequently to the Palace on his account. This was how Kit and Henry first met—on one such visit Kit had been forced to accompany his father and, on entering the royal nursery, saw Henry sitting up in bed looking pale and tired. Henry's gaze went straight to him. 'Hello,' he said with a sudden beaming smile. 'Who are you?' And from that moment on they had been best friends.

9

But Henry's poor health meant he was often sent away on 'rest-cures' in the country. For the last three months he had been 'rest-curing' in Scotland—too far for Hector to fly—and his few ordinary letters to Kit had been brief about ordinary things, because Henry had a fierce Yorkshire nurse who read everything he wrote—which wasn't much because she believed writing tired his brain and was bad for his health. But if Hector was here, it must mean only one thing—that Henry had returned to London.

Sure enough, around Hector's tiny scratchy claw was a note tightly folded and pushed through a little golden ring. Eagerly Kit removed the note, unfolded it many times and began to read—

Dear Kit

> *The fresh air of Scotland nearly killed me.*
> *Ha-ha-ha. So I've been sent back to sooty old*
> *London. Everyone is making their usual fuss over*
> *me and won't let me do a thing for myself.*
> *Grandmama has even forbidden me to run, and I*
> *have to keep taking naps when I'm not a bit tired!*
> *I am so bored. Please come and visit me, tonight if*
> *you can. Remember, come the usual way, I'll be*
> *listening out for your signal.*

Your very best friend
H

PS I really think that tonight I deserve an
adventure!

At the top of the page was a gold-embossed coat of arms around which Henry had drawn flowers and monsters and a pirate ship; an ape-like creature had Kit's name arrowed to it, and underneath the brave soldier who drove back the pirates with his sword, Henry had modestly written 'me'.

Reading the letter made Kit feel so stupidly happy he almost forgot about poor Hector; and when he finally remembered him he saw that Hector had stretched a leathery wing over his head and was half asleep. (For a little foreign bat more used to tropical forests, the journey from Buckingham Palace to Richmond is an extremely long one.) Kit made a fuss of him once more before carrying him across to the wardrobe and hanging him upside down from an empty coathanger, to sleep proper bat fashion. As a special treat, Kit left half an apple upon a pile of crumpled vests, in case Hector should awake hungry.

This done, Kit murmured one word—'Carpet'—and Grandpa Wishbane's flying-carpet leapt up from under the bed, dropping mothballs like big, smooth hailstones (moths being a flying-carpet's particular enemy, along with seagulls and lightning). It hurled itself at Kit, wrapping around him in a show of affection, its excitability put down to the fact that it was not a pedigree flying-carpet, but a mongrel mix of Persian and Chinese, with just a little touch of Axminster.

Kit was too happy even to pretend to be cross with it. 'Behave, Carpet,' he said. 'I need you to carry me to Buckingham Palace. Now make yourself ready.'

As Carpet opened itself out on the floor, Kit pulled on two coats, a pair of gloves, a cap, a scarf, and finally his flying goggles, in readiness for his night flight; then he stepped onto the richly complex and ever-changing patterns of the oriental carpet and sat cross-legged in the middle.

'Rise,' he commanded.

11

Carpet rose, its fringe rippling like the legs of a marching centipede. Kit pointed and the window opened even higher, allowing Carpet to pass smoothly and freely into the night.

Nobody saw Kit slip away from Angel Terrace. Cook was angrily scrubbing the kitchen floor and his father was with Mr Obb. Carpet, guided by unseen stars and magic, flew north over open fields to the river, where it gathered speed until its front edge curled over like a wave. It flew on, over elegant white villas in parklands, and little lanes that seemed to have meandered in from the countryside by mistake. Then came proper streets and the houses grew more crowded together, their chimneys smoking and the wet pavements outside lit with flickering gas lamps. And like grim fortresses amongst the houses stood gasometers and electricity factories; from them buzzing pylons and overground pipes stretching away in all directions. And soon every roof in every street became tied up in a black tangle of electricity cables, telegraph wires, and lines that powered the trams; all of which criss-crossed without plan or order, reminding Kit of the web of a lunatic spider, which crackled and sparked here and there in the darkness.

On sped Carpet, meeting more and more rush-hour traffic as it neared the centre of London.

'Sky-hog!' bellowed Kit at a dirty, cigar-shaped clipper on its way to the main balloondrome at Wembley. Carpet had been forced to swing from its path at the very last moment, probably without the clipper captain even noticing its presence.

But there were more than clippers to watch out for. Hansom aircabs cut back and forth causing slower balloon bicycles to bob in their wake; and blimp omnibuses, their sides covered in gaudy advertisements, jostled one another like fat bathers in a crowded pool, as they chugged out towards the suburbs.

Just then Kit heard a powerful rumbling noise, much louder than any of the other air traffic, and passing from a patch of mist came alongside a mighty Krupp-Zeppelin— metropolis class—belonging to the White Star Line: each of its twenty-four propellers cutting the air with a half sinister swish, and lights shining down the length of its silvery-blue body. In the cabins below, Kit noticed a rich lady in furs staring back at him through a porthole. She was holding up her little dog—a thing no bigger than a muff—and pointing at Kit, speaking all the while to the pampered creature as though it were a small child.

Growing curious to know what was being said about him, Kit whispered to Carpet, 'Fly steady now, Carpet. I'm just going to take a little walk.'

And this is precisely what he did, or rather his *mind* did, across the distance to the cabin where it slipped easily inside the dog's head. The dog's ears flew up and it yelped in surprise.

Shove up, Fido, said Kit, forcing the dog's mind to sit trembling in a shadowy corner.

The woman, unaware of Kit's presence, kissed the dog's nose; when she spoke it was with an American accent. 'No, Tutu, there's no need to bark, Mama's only showing you that cute little English wizard out there all on his lonesome, travelling on that old-time rug of his. Poor mite, I bet he must be half frozen to death—not like us, Tutu darling. Whenever Mrs P. F. Beckerbaker flies it's first class all the way, and she insists on having the heating up full. Who'd be a wizard out there in the cold? Not me, Tutu, that's for sure. Not me . . . '

For some reason her words annoyed Kit much more than they should: he was extremely proud to be a wizard and wanted to be admired for it, not pitied; and as for calling his precious flying-carpet a rug . . . !

Half tempted to persuade the silly little dog into biting

13

her, Kit decided it was more sensible to hurry back to his empty body, where he was able to scowl at the woman instead, alarming her so much that she hurriedly stepped away from the porthole and was gone.

'Isn't nothin' wrong in being a wizard,' said Kit fiercely. 'It's the best thing in the whole world.'

But then, almost reluctantly, he gazed down at Carpet as if for the very first time. As usual its patterns wriggled like intertwining snakes, and squares became rectangles that burst into wavy lines; and the colours flickered and glowed more brightly than embers in a stirring breeze. And yet here and there were bald patches, ancient moth holes and clumsy repairs; and the once golden fringe was slowly unravelling and coming away. But what could anyone expect? Carpet was well over three hundred years old, given to Grandpa Wishbane when he was a young missionary-wizard out in Arabia. In Grandpa Wishbane's day, of course, only witches and wizards flew, and in the eyes of the rest of the world a flying-carpet was marvellously special, as were all things touched by magic. Not today it seemed; and Kit remembered his father's gloomy prediction to Mr Obb. 'Sometimes I believe there will be no place left for magic in the future . . .'

'Oh why did I have to go and overhear *that*?' wailed Kit. 'It's quite spoilt the evening and nothing should be allowed to spoil it now Henry's home.'

By this time Carpet had reached Kensington Gardens. It flew over Round Pond to South Carriage Drive; below, Kit could make out a line of hansom aircabs waiting for business, one just beginning to climb with its 'hired' lamp shining, two slowly descending with their 'hired' lamps dark; and in the distance right to the hazy edge of the city, steeples, smog lighthouses and other familiar landmarks rose from the smoke of the busy streets, the taller buildings speckled with red warning lanterns—and not just for decoration either. Indeed, it would be a great shame if another of London's famous monuments met the same fate as Nelson's Column—renamed Nelson's Stump following a disastrous brush with a blimp several years ago. Over Hyde Park the main windsock hardly stirred and Carpet rode the one breath of wind, dipping down sharply into the gardens of Buckingham Palace to the island in the middle of the ornamental lake. Here, hidden by trees from the back of the palace, Carpet landed safely on the soft earth, and Kit bounded off it pushing up his goggles.

'Stay and roll,' he ordered.

Carpet didn't so much as twitch.

'Oh please, Carpet,' pleaded Kit. 'I shan't be long—I promise.'

Carpet flew up and wrapped itself around him in another affectionate hug. Kit spluttered his protests through his laughter; then Carpet dropped in a crumpled heap about his feet—it straightened itself out, rolled up as tightly as a newspaper and was still.

Although no one was around (certainly not on the island at that time) Kit still felt the need to creep over the fallen leaves, trying not to make a sound. The island was such a mysterious place that Kit always thought it best to act in a mysterious way with it. From the lake a mist was rising and some unseen creature made a splash amongst the reeds . . . and when the sound had faded away a deep silence fell.

Kit made his way to a statue of Pan. It was quite old and mossy and overgrown by surrounding bushes, but there on its face was clearly a leering smile, as if it knew what Kit intended to do. Kit reached out and pushed the statue's hoof. Immediately the plinth made a sound like a grinding millstone and rolled back slowly, uncovering a deep stairway. Kit showed no surprise. And little wonder—he had been a constant visitor to the stairway ever since Henry first revealed it to him.

With a point and word of magic he sent a glow-ball ahead to light the way, the stale air turning it green. Kit followed after, down the damp stone steps and underground, where it was much colder than above and juicy fat slugs squelched under foot.

The glow-ball waited for him, hovering patiently at the bottom of the stairs. Beyond its soft dissolving light ran a brick-lined passage, the vaulted roof high enough to allow Kit to walk without stooping; but where the passage crossed beneath the lake, deep puddles had formed and cold drips fell upon Kit's head; while in the dark, baby stalactites pointed long spindly fingers at him or had sprouted into sinister mushrooms. Then the passage gently sloped upwards until it met another stairway, one Kit knew would take him into the heart of the Palace itself.

He began to climb, breathing in the unpleasant air that tasted of earth and smelt of mildew; he went on climbing until the stairs ended and a blank wall stopped him from going any further. Again Kit knew precisely where to push to make what was this time a small wall panel swing open for him.

'Go.'

He blew out the glow-ball like an unwanted candle and peered through the opening. Before him were the soft red carpets and gilded walls of one of the Palace's main corridors. It was also the place he had to show greatest care, because he needed to cross it in order to reach a little back stairway that led directly to the nursery: the obvious danger was that someone might spot him as he emerged.

Kit looked up and down the corridor several times and saw no one in sight. He was just about to dart forward when he noticed something so unexpected he stopped dead and gasped in disbelief.

'Electric lights!'

Surely he was wrong. He checked again and this time saw wires and switches. He wasn't mistaken at all. Since his last visit to Henry, electric lights had been installed at the Palace. It was *unbelievable*. Before electricity the royal castles and houses had each employed its own special wizard whose only job was to create glow-balls, which servants then led away to rooms as and when they were needed. But electric lights!

Kit stared along the corridor again, this time he wasn't on the look-out for palace servants, he was viewing it with plain disgust. Why, the new lights were all too harsh and glaring—and they were exactly alike! So different to glow-balls which are never the same size or shade of colour—or even tone of warmth. They follow like faithful spaniels and their soft fizzes and crackles are as reassuring to hear as water chuckling around mossy stones. The unnerving silence of electric lights, on the other hand, appears only to make them quite lifeless and dull.

The longer Kit looked the more he found to criticize. The light-bulbs were large, ugly glass spheres which hurt his eyes if he stared at any particular one for too long; and the unrelenting yellow light made every piece of furniture and gilded picture-frame shine in the gaudiest way imaginable. Better to have no lights at all than these, thought Kit having an idea. He pointed mischievously at the nearest set—it grew intensely bright, flickered and suddenly went out. *Tink!*

Feeling honour restored, Kit continued on, slipping across the corridor and up the nursery stair. Halfway up he stopped, gave three sharp taps of his foot, rested, then tapped three times more.

In answer the door at the top of the stairs flew open.

'Kit . . . Kit. Is that you?'

Kit moaned like a ghost.

17

'Have you a belly ache?' asked Henry cheerfully.

'All right, it *is* me,' admitted Kit laughing. 'Is it safe to come up?'

'If you mean am I alone—then yes, yes I am.'

Kit ran up the rest of the stairs and burst into the darkened nursery with a glow-ball blazing at his shoulder like a miniature sun. Apart from Henry, the first thing he noticed was the new electric lights—but at least Henry had been tactful enough to keep them turned off.

'Hello,' said Henry.

'Hello,' said Kit.

They grinned at each other, suddenly shy and at a loss for words. Kit saw that although Henry had grown by an inch or two he remained thin and very pale; while the two dark shadows Kit remembered from last time still lingered under his sleepy blue eyes.

Henry went to speak but Kit shushed him quiet, first setting a silencing spell around the room. Then both boys suddenly flopped down upon Henry's bed and began laughing and talking and joking about nothing at all . . . nothing to anyone else that is.

They had so much news to catch up on. Henry told Kit about landing his first salmon and losing his boots in the heather; about seeing an eagle catch a hare and chasing a stray stag from the vegetable gardens.

'And what about Scottish wizards—what are they like?' Kit demanded to know.

Henry considered a moment.

'Hairy—and they wear kilts . . . so they have to be careful how they ride their broomsticks.'

The two boys fell about helpless with laughter (next door the dour Yorkshire nurse heard nothing so snored on).

Kit had news of his own of course, but first there was one thing he needed to know. Meaningfully he clicked on and off Henry's electric lights several times.

'What are these doing here, eh, Henry?'

Henry grew embarrassed. 'It was Grandmama's idea,' he said. 'Mr Sparks told her they are more efficient.'

Sparks. That was the second time in one evening Kit had heard the name of the Royal Superintendent of Scientific Progress.

'But don't worry,' said Henry brightening up. 'Mr Horgan, the Palace's old glow-ball wizard, has been given a good pension. I should think he's pretty pleased about it—being paid and having nothing to do, that is.'

'That's not the point,' snapped Kit.

Henry saw his friend was serious and grew consoling. 'Up in Scotland it's a different matter,' he said. 'All the old lairds insist on lighting their castles with glow-balls; and they refuse to allow power lines to cross their lands, saying that electricity is the work of the Devil, confusing their hounds and horses . . . Look, Kit, I am sorry, I am really. I wouldn't have changed anything if it were up to me. But Grandmama and Mr Sparks . . . '

'I know it isn't *your* fault,' said Kit gloomily. 'But it's *so* unfair . . . Kings have always had their wizards, and for that matter queens too. They won battles for them, kept their castles safe; and Grandpa Wishbane told me that some ol' weather witch stopped a thunderstorm on your grandma's coronation day, Henry, and . . . and—why are you laughing?'

Henry shook his head. 'Oh, Kit, you sound so funny when you start to lecture me,' he said. 'Before I know it you'll be telling me to wash behind my ears and carry a clean handkerchief.'

Kit went to give him a friendly punch but stopped himself.

Henry glared. 'I'm not made of china, you know. I won't break.'

'Sorry,' said Kit looking away.

19

'Never mind, I'm sorry too, about the electricity, I mean.' Henry's old grin sprang back. 'Hey, you haven't told me any news about the gang. How is everyone? Will we be seeing them tonight for an adventure?'

'If you're not too tired . . . tired from travelling, that is.'

Henry stood up, haughtily brushing off the remark. 'I'm not in the least tired. Now hurry up and do your magic, Kit, and we can be gone.'

Kit understood perfectly what he meant and while Henry pulled on his outdoor clothes, he spoke and pointed at the bed. The air cracked and the bed covers rose as if someone lay underneath them; presently a ghostly sleeping face took shape on the pillow.

'Pooh, looks nothing like me,' complained Henry.

'Too right,' agreed Kit. 'Far too handsome.' Yet really he was extremely proud of his night wraith; it was definitely good enough to fool whichever of the servants poked his head around the door later on to check if Henry was sleeping soundly.

The two boys playfully jostled each other down the stairway until Kit suddenly remembered something and stopped.

'Oh,' he said hardly able to hide his smugness. 'If you happen to run into that ol' magic hater, Sparks, you best tell him that some of his wonderful electric lights aren't working. Must be a loose wire or summat,' he added in all innocence.

'Shh, you idiot!' hissed Henry at the bottom door. 'You'll be telling him yourself soon if you make any more noise. Can't you hear? He's out in the corridor at this very moment.'

Sure enough now he came to listen, Kit heard voices. 'That's Grandmama with him,' whispered Henry. 'And if she catches me here with you I shall be packed straight

20

back to Scotland on the royal airbarge, and you probably won't set eyes on me ever again.'

'Let me see,' said Kit pushing past; before Henry was able to prevent him he eased open the door by an inch.

The corridor was as before, gilt and silver and brashly lit, after the darkness of the stairway it almost made Kit wince. Then he caught sight of a little plump figure dressed in black satin, her white wavy hair swept back into a tight bun. Here was Her Majesty herself, strolling arm in arm with a tall, severe looking man.

'That's Sparks,' said Henry, and Kit stared fiercely at him, searching for things to dislike.

Now he looked closer, Kit saw that Mr Sparks wasn't nearly so tall as he first thought and really it was more in the way of the Queen being particularly short. Reluctantly Kit decided that the Royal Superintendent of Scientific Progress wasn't especially ugly, but neither were his looks what might be called pleasing. Beyond a curl or two he was practically bald on top, although to make up for the loss he possessed a magnificent set of woolly mutton-chop whiskers, which swept down to an equally impressive moustache; and his dense eyebrows met over his nose. Beneath the shadow of his brow, two grey eyes moved restlessly in an alert wolf-like way. As he walked he sucked upon an enormous cigar and his tie-pin, Kit noticed with strong disapproval, was a tiny solid silver spanner which winked slyly in the electric lights.

Just then the Queen was speaking.

'I am an old lady now, of course, Mr Sparks. Yes—yes, you cannot say it's not true, but I do consider myself very modern and far-seeing.'

'Let no man doubt it, Ma'am,' replied Mr Sparks, his voice rich and deep. 'Very modern indeed. That is why I believe my main task is to press ahead and build for you the most up-to-date underground railway in the world.' He sucked hard upon his cigar. 'It's a scandal, but here we are in the greatest city ever to have existed, yet at every turn its roads are jammed solid and the skies above are thronged with flying machines. The way forward, if you'll permit me to say, Ma'am, is to tunnel directly beneath the city's streets and join every part of it to a fast, efficient underground railway that will be the envy of all other nations.'

'Surely London already has an underground railway, Mr Sparks; is it not good enough?'

'In short, Ma'am, no. Why, the trains still run on steam so each journey half chokes its passengers and ruins their clothes with soot. The need is for modernization—and that means electricity and electric trains; after that a great many more stations which must be built everywhere— even one here at Buckingham Palace.'

'Gracious, what a thought,' said the Queen. 'An underground station at the Palace. Won't the windows rattle?'

Mr Sparks didn't answer. 'These are modern times, Ma'am,' he said firmly, 'and modern times demand modern ways.'

'Ah, progress,' sighed the Queen. 'We do move so very fast nowadays. How my poor, dear Albert would have enjoyed it, he did so much love the latest ideas.'

At the Queen's mention of her long-dead husband, Mr Sparks flicked cigar ash onto the carpet and Kit noticed his eyes roll up and glance at the ceiling, as if sick of hearing of the Prince, but he said, 'I'm sure he did, Ma'am. After all, wasn't it Prince Albert himself who organized and had built our magnificent Temple of Science at Kensington?'

The Queen nodded and tears filled her eyes. 'Dear Albert . . . This is why I am so keen on science and for progress, you understand, Mr Sparks'; and she added in a whisper, 'My Albert would have approved so much.' And she gave a sad little smile.

With that they strolled on, out of Kit's line of vision, leaving him scowling and feeling extremely peeved.

Neither one had noticed his broken lights.

Chapter Three

By the time Kit and Henry reached the island and climbed out of the secret passageway, a frost had begun to bite; hairy ice crystals sparkled on blades of grass and old soggy leaves were turned crisp and white. In the distance through the bare trees a watchman's lantern blinked at them.

Kit noticed Henry give a violent shiver, but Henry shrugged it off and said half angrily, 'I'm all right, I tell you. Now where's Carpet? How I've missed the daffy old thing.'

Kit whistled softly and Carpet crashed down on them from the branches above, giving Henry a breathtaking rug-hug. When it was calmer, Kit clambered aboard, sitting cross-legged as before but to one side to leave enough room for Henry, who preferred to lie on his belly, hold on to the front edge, and peer down at the world passing below him.

The moment his friend was settled beside him, Kit gave the command to rise—their destination the gasometers by St Pancras station.

Carpet lifted effortlessly from the ground and when high enough found a southerly breeze to carry it like a river carries a little boat, only much much faster. Rush hour over, the traffic was noticeably lighter than before, just a few scattered blimps; and with nothing to get in Carpet's way, it flew straight and smooth.

'Look—look—Piccadilly Circus!' cried Henry excitedly as soon as he saw the bright dancing lights. Kit watched him, quietly amused; it was easy to forget Henry had been away for so long.

'And there . . . ' shouted Henry pointing. 'The British Museum. Do you remember, Kit, that night we squeezed through a skylight and went to see the wizened old mummies in their coffins?'

'I remember your teeth rattling with fright,' said Kit.

'Not mine—that must have been your knobbly knees knocking together.'

'Well anyway, we both jumped out of our skins when that watchman went and shone his lamp in our faces, before chasing us out. I thought we'd never shake him off.'

They laughed at the memory of their narrow escape for the rest of the way to St Pancras, which suddenly loomed up before them, its illuminated clock glowing like a harvest moon. They flew over it and Kit nodded down. Steam trains and carriages stood idly at platforms beneath the vast glass canopy; while behind the station's brightness stood the solid, dark shapes of the gasometers.

Business there tonight was slack, no more than a couple of balloon bicycles waiting to fill up with gas. Henry, however, didn't notice even these, his gaze was too keenly fixed to the gasometers' flat tops. Presently he saw what he searched for.

First one, two, three, four . . . and finally five broomsticks lifted like thistledown into the air from the nearest of the big, cast-iron tanks. For Henry's sake Kit was glad the whole gang had managed to make it tonight. He waved and the posse of brooms streaked towards him, led by Fin, a big beefy lad, who in spite of the sharp cold was dressed as always in a collarless shirt and waistcoat, his pork-pie hat set at an angle on the side of his head. Close behind came Alfie laughing as usual; then Gus, and

Pixie—who was Gus's twin sister and wore her hair nearly as short as his; and right at the back on an almost twigless besom was Tommy, as desperate to keep up as he was to grow up and fill out his much patched hand-me-down clothes. Kit's passenger was spotted straight away.

'Hen—ry!'

The gang seemed as genuinely pleased to see Henry as Kit had been—yet there was no allowance for him being Queen Victoria's grandson. No hats whipped off, no bows or the like. He might have come from a rough part of the East End as they all did. To them he was simply Henry; it was what Henry liked best about the gang, that and the fact no one treated him as an invalid . . . although sometimes they good-naturedly teased him because he wasn't a wizard.

Slowly the gang circled the flying-carpet, Gus practising leg swings over his broom handle like a circus acrobat and grinning up at Henry for his approval. Then Fin gave his own broom a sharp kick with his heels and rode up close alongside Carpet.

'Grand to have you back with us, Henry, we missed you, you old dog,' he said, reaching over to shake Henry's hand.

Kit scowled, perhaps a little jealous. Or perhaps he didn't like the way Fin acted so big, as if it fell to him to be the gang's natural leader. This time Kit said nothing, just glanced away.

'We was all thinking that you weren't coming tonight,' said Fin nodding towards Kit.

'Said I was, didn't I?' replied Kit coldly.

Fin shrugged. 'We was just flying up the West End.'

'We're gonna play *soot bombs*,' piped up Tommy, blinking excitedly through his thick, second-hand spectacles. 'Ain't that so, Fin?'

Fin smiled and nodded.

Kit scowled again. Soot bombs was a game he'd invented: it was played by dropping a mild exploding spell down a promising looking chimney, before speeding to the street below for a good viewing place, from where—with pretend innocence—they could watch the surprised, soot-covered occupants of the house stumble out, coughing and spluttering. Sometimes the gang offered to make good the mess and considered itself cheap at sixpence! Kit had quite a gift for games, his games were best by far—like *bobby hatting*. That is, flying so low and fast over a policeman that his helmet blew over his eyes. Now, thought Kit bitterly, Fin was going to take the gang off and play one of *his* games without him. He was about to point out who the gang's chief games-maker-upperer was, when Henry spoke.

'Soot bombs might be fun to play,' he said in a slow doubtful tone. 'That is if we hadn't something else— something better to do.'

Kit shot him a look and saw the gleam of mischief in his eyes. What was he up to? he wondered. Henry smiled at him and went on.

'It's just that I happen to know something. I happen to know that the Tsar of all the Russians has sent my Grandmama a present.'

'What's a futzer?' asked Tommy.

'*Tsar*,' said Kit grandly. It's what them ol' Russians call their king.'

'Tell us then, Henry,' said Pixie leaning forward on her broomstick. 'I like presents though I ain't never on the receiving end of too many. What's your gran got off this old king of the Russians?'

Henry paused, glancing around mysteriously at their waiting faces. Then he smiled and whispered, 'Only some of the most dangerous creatures in the whole world.'

'Sharks!' screamed Tommy. 'It's sharks!'

Henry shot him a regal look. Alfie laughed. The moment was spoilt.

'Shan't tell you if you don't want to know.'

'Aw, go on,' said Pixie; and Kit had to admit he was more than a little interested too.

Only when he was sure of their complete and utmost attention did Henry breathe out a single word.

'*Werewolves.*'

It released all kinds of fireworks in the way of excited exclamations.

Henry nodded eagerly. 'True as I'm sitting before you now, the Tsar of all the Russians has given Grandmama a pack of rare Siberian werewolves. They arrived by secret shipment on Tuesday so as not to alarm the city; and they're one of the reasons I was so desperate to be back in London—I've been pleading all week to come.' He clutched his heart dramatically. 'And I swear to you I shall die if I don't see my first living werewolf right this very night.'

'We can see 'em after we've been soot bombing up West,' said Fin. He was shouted down at once. Kit smiled to himself. Everyone wanted to visit the Queen's new werewolves.

'But it'll be dangerous,' warned Henry. He gestured at the shining mist. 'Tonight's a full moon, and everyone knows werewolves have to hunt when the moon is full.'

'Gawd, he's making my hair bristle!' hollered Gus, and Alfie laughed and bayed like a wolf. Pixie was so excited she could hardly keep her broomstick still.

'What we waiting for?' she cried. 'Let's fly!'

'Where?' demanded Tommy, worried in case he fell behind and got lost. 'Are they being kept at London Zoo?'

Alfie laughed. 'Ain't penguins or even crocodiles we going to see this time, Tommy,' he said. 'Those are common animals, although, granted, not a regular sight on the Whitechapel Road. The Queen has her special creatures like the werewolves and she keeps 'em at the Tower. Ain't that so, Henry? Which means we have to watch out for them Beefeaters who guard it, or I daresay they might turn out as fierce as the werewolves if they catches us there.'

'Huh, first they have to catch us,' said Kit, and to show how fast he could go he ordered Carpet to fly at full magic to the Tower of London.

The brooms gave chase, Tommy wailing, 'Wait for me!' but then Tommy was always wailing that. Very soon they reached the Thames, made bright with strings of electric lights—its bridges too. First Blackfriars Bridge, then Southwark Bridge, and on to the grand mansions that stood solidly upon the back of old London Bridge. On any other occasion they would have lingered at the Icelandic Embassy in order to pay a special visit to the ambassador's pet polar bear, which he kept in a cage on the roof, but tonight they didn't so much as slow down for it; and Fin gazed wistfully at the ambassador's many inviting chimneys.

'Not too late to play at least one game of soot bombs,' he said.

Nobody listened.

They sped down the Thames, passing tugs and barges tied up upon both banks and seeing up ahead Tower Bridge grow clearly visible; a number of sail-and-propeller liners moored behind, bound on the morning tide for India, Australia, or South America.

Quite unexpectedly the moon slid from the mists and surprised them with its brightness; the solid black river straight away transformed into a living thing of silver tipped wavelets and swirling eddies; and long wet sand banks glistened like the backs of eels.

And then finally they reached the Tower, and who

arrived first and who arrived second was forgotten as the gang became a close group once more, the brooms riding up and down on the damp river breeze. Apart from a tiny gleaming window here and there, the Tower refused to be softened by moonlight or appear in any way welcoming: its walls were black and dismal, and at points patrolled by uniformed yeomen (Beefeaters, the gang called them).

'Gaw', don'it look a downright scary heap,' said Gus.

Pixie glanced at him scornfully. 'Well, if you're getting cold feet, Gus Betts, you may as well take yourself back home and help our ma peel the spuds.' Like most twins they were both the best of friends and the worst of enemies.

Gus snorted at the very suggestion. 'Cold feet? Me? Nah, I was just saying, that's all. Anyhow I wouldn't leave my little sister here without me.'

Pixie rode her broom away from his to show she didn't need anyone taking care of her, thank you very much. Then Kit addressed the gang.

'We stick together—right—and fly low,' he said. 'If spotted we take off like rockets in different directions and meet up again back at the gasometers. If anyone gets caught they don't breathe a single word about the others. Understood?—Gang honour.'

'Gang honour,' they repeated solemnly—then everyone spat in the Thames.

'They can lock me up in the Tower if they catches me,' said Gus.

'They prob'ly will. Now quick, follow me while the Beefeaters are furthest apart.' Kit threw Fin a last triumphant look as Carpet led the line of broomsticks so low over Traitors Gate that any one of the riders could have reached down and without the slightest effort touched the sooty moss growing on its battlements. Then they crept over a circular tower and came at last inside the castle walls. Had they not had Henry to guide the way, they could have easily found the Queen's menagerie from the grunts and squawks arising just then, the creatures possibly sensing the arrival of their magic.

'Land us here please, Kit,' said Henry, and Kit put Carpet down on a dark patch of grass before a metal cage.

'We're all here behind you,' whispered a voice. It was Fin.

In the cage something very large moved, drawing the youngsters immediately to the bars.

'I'll raise us a glow-ball,' said Tommy.

'No!' snapped Kit and Henry together. 'You want the Beefeaters to know we're here?'

As their eyes grew used to the darkness, they began to make out a strange gloomy creature perched in a dead tree. It was bird-like in outline yet as big as a man, with a cruel hooked beak and a lion's mane.

'That's the Persian griffin,' whispered Kit, who remembered seeing it during a previous—*educational*—visit with his father.

'Nasty piece of meat, ain't he?' said Alfie.

The griffin turned, seeming to understand Alfie's meaning if not his precise words. It opened and closed its beak with a powerful crack, showing how easily it might break a man's thigh bone in two—a boy's . . . well that would be even less bother.

At this the gang was persuaded to hurry on to the next cage, which was larger by far than the griffin's, and here even Tommy in his secondhand spectacles had no difficulty recognizing a dragon when he saw one.

'Gaw'—how he stinks!' said Pixie holding her nose.

Smeltz, the Queen's dragon, lay on a nest of smashed planks, breathing with slow, rumbling snorts: a creature of relative harmlessness since the removal of its main fire gland, although a little smoke still trickled from between

31

its thick leathery lips, and curled up from either nostril, past a tethering ring. With disinterested, half closed eyes it regarded its audience for a while, then suddenly shook the dust from its stubby wings as if trying to startle it . . . dragons have a very odd sense of humour. This particular one was as large as an air-cab and extremely old. On its claws were hastily scratched the names or initials of those who in past times had been brave enough to approach the dragon while it slept. Kit peered closely and read as many as he could. 'E. P. 1676 . . . V. J. D. 1744 . . . '; more intriguing was the beginning of a name—*Edwa*—followed by a long scratch. Kit wondered if the Edward in question took fright and fled, or whether Smeltz had simply awoken and eaten him. In olden days dragons had eaten whole villages of people, so a single man would hardly be more than a passing snack. At the back of Smeltz's cage was an old dented suit of armour from the Tower's armoury, given to the dragon to play with in the same way a cloth mouse is given to a kitten. The helmet, crushed and plumeless, lay pinned beneath Smeltz's heavy claws.

'Eeh—how disgusting!' shrieked Pixie suddenly. For as they stood watching, one of the dragon's scales lifted like a lid on a boiling saucepan and a blood-swollen dragon-flea the size of a sparrow popped out. Before it was able to dart for cover under a different scale, Smeltz slowly turned its massive head and caught the flea with a long, lazy lick of its blue tongue. Its swallow made the ground tremble.

Alfie laughed. Pixie said she felt sick, and Tommy wailed, 'I don't want to see a dragon, I want to see werewolves,' because Smeltz frightened him so much.

'Come on then, they must be close by,' said Kit.

'What's up with Henry?' asked Gus.

Kit turned and saw Henry leaning against the bars of the dragon's cage, ghostly pale in the moonlight. But before he could speak, Henry jumped up straight and said angrily, 'What do you mean?—I'm fine. Now are we going to find these werewolves or not?'

So they left the dragon to its fleas and crossed to a likely looking enclosure nearby. This was surrounded by a ten foot high wall set into which were a number of tiny barred openings; in front of each opening, blocking the view inside, was a sign, and on each was written in large red warning letters: 'Highly Dangerous—on no account approach'.

Like all warnings they had ever met with, the gang didn't consider that these new ones could in any way be meant for them. They swarmed up to the wall and tore down the signs, anxiously standing on tiptoes to glimpse what was forbidden and supposed to be hid.

Quite by chance Kit found he had a good view, but despite searching hard at first saw nothing of interest, merely a patch of unlevel ground with rocks scattered here and there, and the outer wall of the Tower rising much higher behind. Then, where the shadows lay deepest, he caught a slight movement—and then the cool gleam of an eye. Then he saw grey, steaming breath . . . and then at last sighted the werewolves . . . *six* werewolves, standing together in a silent pack, watching him far more closely than he watched them.

When his first shivers had past, Kit had to admit to a sense of disappointment. If he hadn't known, he would have sworn these were just ordinary wolves—admittedly larger than usual and more powerfully muscled at the shoulder, but not the nightmare creatures he had always supposed them to be. However, as the werewolves sensed the warm blood of other living things and soundlessly moved out into a shaft of white moonlight, Kit gasped, understanding perfectly why werewolves are to be feared.

Sinister. That was the only word to describe them.

Sinister. It was the half human expression on each werewolf's face that Kit found so unsettling, and the way they often and quickly changed. Amongst the pack Kit easily read the unmistakable looks of slyness, cleverness, and suspicion; as well as cruelty and greed. And as he stared, one werewolf slowly winked a cold blue eye at him, not in a friendly manner, but as if marking him out. For these were hunting animals and this was a full moon; and their jaws were pure wolf, with one important exception. Towards the front of its muzzle each werewolf had two long fangs as sharp as assassins' knives. *Sinister,* Kit reminded himself needlessly . . .

'I don't think I like it here,' yelped Tommy suddenly leaping back, no longer able to meet a werewolf stare for stare.

'Ga'wan,' sneered Fin. 'Ain't nothing to be scared of but a load of big, ugly mutts.'

'But *bloodsuckers,* Fin!' Tommy blinked wide-eyed through his owlish spectacles.

'Well, I ain't scared of 'em, bloodsuckers or not.'

'That's just wind for your sail,' said Gus.

'No it's not,' returned Fin. He proudly prodded his broad chest with his thumb. 'I tell you I've seen scarier sights walk past my house at night.'

Alfie laughed at him, the others jeered. But worse, far worse, was Kit who just watched on and smiled as if pitying him.

'Right, I'll prove it—I'll shame the lot of you.'

With a word of magic he leapt up twice his height onto the wall of the werewolf enclosure, throwing out his arms for balance as he landed. 'Not using my magic now,' he called. 'Just you watch, I'll walk to the very end all by myself.'

The others shouted up to him in dismay, even Kit. 'Come on down, Fin—this is stupid!' Fin ignored them, edging his way forward, carefully placing one boot in front of the other. Down on the opposite side of the wall the werewolves bristled with agitation. To their mind it was as if their food were tormenting them and not the other way round—as they believed was the proper behaviour between diner and dined-upon. Savage snarls reached Fin's ears, and the one time he glanced down he met six pairs of furious, ice cold eyes and felt them willing him to drop.

At last he reached the end of the wall and proudly raised his pork-pie hat. Big show off, thought Kit as he jumped down: this time it was Fin who did the smiling. His challenge was wordless.

'My turn,' said Kit. He sprang up onto the wall and letting go of his magic wobbled so dangerously that Tommy turned away with a hand over his eyes.

'Don't worry, I'm fine,' said Kit and smiled.

The werewolves circled tightly around each other like a whirlpool of coarse, bristling fur—yet Kit's friends watched in total silence as he pointed his toe ready to take a first step. Surprisingly he found it harder than he'd imagined because much of the wall lay in the shadow of a tree, and the shadow made it difficult to judge where to set down his foot with any measure of certainty, especially with the brickwork at the top so broken and uneven.

'Grrrr . . . ' The biggest werewolf fought free of the pack and bounded up on a boulder. Kit felt its piercing blue eyes fix upon him and swore too he could feel its hot gusty breath upon his face. He swayed.

'Oh, be careful, Kit,' he heard Henry utter.

He took another step and breathed out—then quickly took three more steps in a row. His confidence growing steadily he pressed on until he reached the end; swiftly jumping down. Despite the cold he was amazed to find he was sweating and that his heart beat excitedly in his chest.

Fin pulled an unconvincing smile while the others crowded around patting Kit on the back. Nobody noticed Henry begin to climb up by himself.

'Hen-ry!'

Kit saw him first and rushed over to the foot of the wall as Henry pulled himself upright on unsteady legs, his face ashen against the dark night.

'Henry, you come down this second. Y'hear? Come down now or I'll never let you come witching with us again—that's a promise!'

Henry stood still, arms outstretched, his breath coming in rapid white clouds. 'Stop telling me what to do, Kit Stixby,' he said loudly. 'I'm tired of people always telling me what to do. I'm tired—'

Suddenly he seemed to buckle at the knees. He let out a gasp of horror and his eyes jerked fully open. And snatching desperately at the air he slowly tipped backwards into the werewolves' den.

Chapter Four

For one long terrible moment nothing moved, no breath of wind or sound or thought inside anyone's head; while the very moonlight seemed to turn harsh and freeze upon the metal bars. Henry lay perfectly still on the floor of the werewolves' den, while the werewolves with lowered heads glowered at him in hostile suspicion, thinking this some kind of trap and puzzling over why the human's blood smelt so thin and strange (a medicine type smell if only they knew it), not at all like the thick, rich gravy they craved. Kit's mouth hung open. But it was as if he had forgotten how to shout; his legs were heavy and his arms hung uselessly at his sides, but he simply did not want or know how to use them any more, because if he did he knew he must also do something and it was impossible to think what.

Then a little way away Smeltz gave a loud spluttering snort and the spell was finally broken, everything found its voice again and remembered how to move. Kit led the frantic dash to the barred openings, everyone calling out Henry's name. On the other side of the wall, the werewolves happily let loose a long, chilling howl. Soon it would be their time to drink, but not yet: first places had to be jostled for—feeding time had its strict rules, even for werewolves. Savagely the biggest animal struck out and growled the others into order; and the werewolves slunk past each other with slavering jaws and horrible wild eyes.

'Henry! Henry!' shouted his friends desperately.

It was useless—Henry lay quite motionless, his head upon one arm and his eyes closed. Then the worst of all possible things happened. The great brute that led the pack turned and leapt straight at him.

'Rarroooow!'

Its fangs sank deep into Henry's arm and immediately there was blood.

Yet before it could properly drink, or the others rush forward for their share, a blistering white light dropped from the sky, singeing the fur of the two nearest werewolves. Instantly the pack's greedy confidence changed to fearful panic: the ones pushed to last in the feeding line led the scramble to the shadows, snarling as the light dimmed.

Kit turned to Fin and Alfie on one side, and Gus, Pixie, and Tommy on the other, wondering which one had managed to overcome his fears enough to use magic—but he found them staring back at him in equal bewilderment.

Still, he did not have to wait long for the mystery to be answered. Into the moonlight came limping an immense, scowling female in a long fur coat. On her head perched a tiny hat like a dish of wilting flowers, and her old flying shawl was trimmed with crows' down. In one hand she gripped a folded umbrella created from the same crows' stiff black wing feathers, its bone handle carved to the likeness of a bird; hooked over the other arm was a wicker basket brimming with dragon scales as big as dinner plates, as well as many other sheddings and snippets from the rest of the animals. That she was a witch was too obvious to say; and what she had gathered in her basket, Kit realized, were the soon to be ingredients for her enchantments.

'Boys—silly little boys!' she said, limping right up to

them and glaring almost as savagely as the werewolves. Pixie half opened her mouth to explain she wasn't—and never had been—a boy, but the sweep of the old woman's glare caught her and she thought better of it.

'Foolish boys. Not-a-thought-in-their-empty-heads boys. *Crazy* boys!'

The old woman slammed down her basket and pointed her feathery umbrella through the bars of the werewolves' den. Henry slowly rose from the ground. Seeing an easy meal begin to slip through its claws, the chief werewolf sprang forward with a growl; but a point from the old witch's free hand sent a crackling flame of raw magic to scorch its nose and it speedily lost its appetite.

'Lunatic boys. Bound-for-Bedlam boys. Bats-and-cuckoo boys . . .'

The old woman chuntered angrily as Henry floated over the enclosure wall and landed safely at her feet.

His friends dashed forwards.

'W-ah—he ain't murdered is he?' wailed Tommy, and Gus wiped his nose on the back of his sleeve.

The old woman pulled them off and roughly bundled them away. She placed her fingers on the side of Henry's head.

'Well?' demanded Kit anxiously.

'Hmm. He'll live to be foolish another day, I suppose,' answered the old woman.

She gazed up at their weary, concerned faces. 'Leave him with me, silly little boys,' she said a touch less harshly. 'Go home and never come to this place again, or next time I might let the werewolves suck you dry, and I mean what I say.'

Nobody moved.

'*Go*—before I set one of my special curses snapping at your heels!'

39

Tommy, scared out of his wits, hopped on his broomstick so quickly he nearly fell off it again; the others followed more slowly, hovering on their brooms but not wanting to leave.

'But you promise Henry'll get better. You promise, missus!' called Pixie tearfully.

'I've not lost a patient to a werewolf bite yet. Go—you waste my time.'

'Come on,' said Fin gloomily. 'Won't do us any favours if we gets into more trouble.' He led the line of brooms away as if to a funeral.

The old witch meantime got down on her clicky knees and began drawing a feather across Henry's forehead. She didn't look up but knew that Kit was lurking behind.

'W-e-ll?'

'It's just that . . . well, I have a flying-carpet and I wondered, that is . . . will it do for carrying Henry?' He swallowed heavily, adding, 'Aunt Pearl . . . '

The old woman twisted round her head, suddenly and deeply curious. 'Charles's boy? Can't remember your name, but always knew you'd come to no good. Was right, wasn't I?'

'Y-yes . . . I suppose.'

'Well, don't just stand there filling your pockets with moonbeams, go fetch this useful article of yours. A werewolf bite is a nasty business, you know.'

Kit summoned Carpet and it arrived as playful as a puppy. It might have given Aunt Pearl a friendly hug had she not ordered it to *sit* in no uncertain terms. Henry was arranged upon it. He moved restlessly, now and again crying out as if from a nightmare.

'That'll be the poison in the werewolf's spit,' explained Aunt Pearl matter-of-factly. 'Now I suppose you must tell me this unfortunate child's address so we can take him home.'

Kit took a large breath.

'Buckingham Palace,' he managed to say with difficulty. 'Henry . . . is the Queen's grandson.'

If she was impressed by such matters, Aunt Pearl didn't show it.

'My,' she said to herself, 'you Stixbys never did do things by halves.' She plonked her umbrella and wicker basket next to Henry; then hitching up her skirts she stepped aboard Carpet and made herself comfortable.

'I'll see your friend safely back to the Palace. You better take my broomstick and fetch your father.' She sniffed. 'We may have had our differences in the past, but he's an extremely able witch doctor. Oh, and listen here, my no-good nephew, that broomstick has served me perfectly well for nigh on forty years; I shall be most displeased to find it ridden into splinters in a single night. Off with you now.'

Clutching her hat and flattening the wilted flowers even further, Aunt Pearl barked at Carpet to rise. It rose heavily, sagging in the middle, the extra weight (mainly Aunt Pearl's, it must be said) making it sluggish in the air. As it crossed the wall, Kit heard his aunt complain loudly how she never did like flying-carpets, but she supposed they were brash and showy enough for the Stixbys.

When she was gone, Kit felt a sharp poke in his back. He turned. It was Aunt Pearl's broomstick, as bossy as she was. 'Yes, I better go,' murmured Kit, although he did not look forward to facing his father.

Dr Stixby paced up and down in front of Kit in his dark panelled study.

'I cannot believe I am hearing this,' he said—speaking the words not for the first time since Kit's return to Angel Terrace, nor would it be the last time either; still, at least this was preferable to his long grim silences.

41

Kit blinked back some tears. 'It's not *all* my fault, I tried to stop him. I really did.'

'Stop him?' Dr Stixby spun on the soles of his feet to face him. 'You had no right being at such a dangerous place to begin with—and certainly no right involving the Queen's grandson.'

Kit pulled his mouth tight and blinked even harder against tears. *He cares more about Henry because he's a royal than he does about me—his own son,* he thought bitterly. *Why, if he didn't spend every evening locked away and peering down his precious microscope at stupid twigs and leaves, then this might never have happened in the first place.* The more Kit brooded about it, the more ready he became to blame his father.

'Fetch my green top hat,' ordered Dr Stixby at last. 'I'll get my black bag.' And he added firmly, 'We can talk more about this later.'

It was midnight when two broomstick riders were seen to rise from the shadowy back garden of Dr Stixby's house. The sky was translucent and the roofs they flew over shone with frost and moonlight. Kit wasn't the least bit tired and he managed to ignore the cold, finding the silence between him and his father far more chilling. But they had nothing to say to each other: Kit was too miserable for words, and he knew his father was too angry. So they flew in silence over a hushed and frosty London until they sighted Buckingham Palace.

As soon as they landed a footman showed Kit and his father to the royal nursery. However, as they approached they saw the Queen and Stafford Sparks standing in front of its closed door. Dr Stixby slipped off his emerald green hat and clutched it to his chest. Kit hung back slightly—both the Queen and Mr Sparks staring at him.

'Tell me, witch doctor,' said the Queen icily. 'Is this the child that led astray poor dear Henry?'

'I'm afraid . . . ' faltered Dr Stixby. 'This is my son, Kit—Christopher.'

'He doesn't look much like a villain,' sneered Mr Sparks. 'But then looks never do tell the whole story.'

'His heart is good,' protested Dr Stixby feebly. 'It's just that mischief comes rather too easily to him.'

'*Mischief*.' The Queen stiffened. 'Poor Henry was nearly devoured tonight by a pack of savage werewolves. That is beyond mischief, witch doctor. Far beyond.'

'Treason I do believe, Ma'am, in the eyes of the law,' smiled Mr Sparks innocently.

Kit didn't care about any of that, he just wanted news of his friend, but when he tried to force himself to speak, the words became stuck to the insides of his mouth. At last with great effort he managed to say, 'H-how is Henry?'

'*Poor* Henry is recovering,' said the Queen, looking away so as not to speak to such a wretch directly. 'And all thanks to the modern approach of dear Mr Sparks here.'

'Regular electric shocks,' said Mr Sparks. 'That will see him through.'

Dr Stixby was horrified. 'But werewolf poisoning needs to be treated with extreme caution. Please, Ma'am, I beg you to think again. I have in my bag a trusted balm that—'

'Electric shocks,' said Mr Sparks firmly. 'One every three hours. It causes the blood to flow faster, washing out impurities. Science, you see, Stixby, not the out-dated mumbo-jumbo you preach.'

Kit's face turned red and hot, and he flew into a fury on his father's behalf.

'Well, I think your mouldy old science sounds a hundred times worse than any werewolf's bite. And . . . and everyone knows magic is a million times better than your stupid electricity!'

This time his words slipped out of him as if greased, and Kit shocked even himself. The Queen, Mr Sparks, and his father stared at him harshly.

'Silence, Kit,' hissed Dr Stixby.

At that moment Henry must have awoken and heard their voices. 'Kit . . . Kit,' he called. 'Is that you out there?'

'I forbid—' began the Queen. But before she was able to finish, Kit leapt forward. He darted around her black, billowing skirts and dodging Mr Sparks's grabbing hands, burst into the nursery. Henry was struggling to pull himself up onto his pillow, his arm bound in a large white bandage. By his bedside stood an ugly machine on wheels, its front covered with dials and switches; and thick rubber-covered wires coiled from its sides like snakes about to strike.

Kit ran to Henry who had a half wild look about him.

'Kit, is your father here?' he wailed. 'Tell him to bring his magic to make me better, electricity hurts too much—'

'It is for your own good, sir,' growled Mr Sparks, hooking his arm around Kit's neck and dragging him away.

'You leave me alone!' shouted Kit, kicking back as hard as he could and striking his shin.

With a moan Mr Sparks collapsed to the floor, and a firmer hand then seized Kit—this time it was his father.

'*Enough*, Kit. For heaven's sake remember where you are.'

Unused to such rough and tumble, the Queen wavered close to fainting. 'Please . . . please . . . poor Henry . . . ' she reminded them. Then growing more angry she turned upon Dr Stixby.

'Witch doctor,' she said in a voice both trembling and terrible to hear. 'We have no further need of your services

44

tonight. In fact they will not be called upon now or ever again—you have done *quite* enough. Please be so good as to leave and not trouble yourself to call again. I appoint Mr Sparks to take full charge in your place.'

Mr Sparks, grovelling on the floor, paused to look up in triumph.

'Magic is dead,' he declared.

Grave faced, Dr Stixby strode through the Palace, Kit trailing a little way behind more miserable than ever before. He noticed that his father didn't put on his emerald green top hat, seeing no point now he was no longer the Queen's witch doctor. Endlessly he turned it in his hands.

'G'night to you, sir,' said a young porter cheerily.

Dr Stixby didn't reply.

Outside, as they walked to their brooms in stony silence, a large awkward figure waited. She came limping up as soon as they appeared.

'Charles, I've heard rumours—'

'You were listening at the window, more like,' replied Dr Stixby coldly. 'Meddling as you usually do.'

'You are upset, Charles, that is natural, so I shall let your remark pass me by. I was concerned, that is all. But if you think concern the same as meddling—'

'I'm sorry,' said Dr Stixby with effort.

'Tell me,' said Aunt Pearl, 'do you still live at that ridiculously large house out in Richmond?' (Dr Stixby nodded.) 'Good, then I know the way. Well, no use giving me that lightning-struck look, Charles, we must decide what is to be done.'

Aunt Pearl took back her broomstick, and after examining it for damage in a most obvious way, hooked her brolly and basket over the handle and hovered on it a

45

few feet off the ground. Dr Stixby and Kit meanwhile took to their own broom and carpet. Like a lot of elderly witches, Aunt Pearl preferred to ride her broom sidesaddle—with one hand pressed down on her hat. She did not approve of speed.

Somewhere on the journey home Kit must have fallen asleep, and Carpet, sensing how cold and unhappy he was, curled itself around him hugging him tight. Dr Stixby gazed across with a sad look in his eyes; he wondered if it should be a father's work to do such hugging.

Kit awoke in the dark to find himself safely back home in his own bed. For a brief moment he wondered whether the night's adventure had been part of an elaborate dream. He even pretended it had, as all the while a horrible empty feeling inside him kept telling him it was otherwise; and he had just to think of Henry for fresh tears to flow.

He sat up. Light beneath his door showed that a glow-ball still burned in the hallway. His father couldn't yet be in bed, prevented no doubt by Aunt Pearl. What could the pair of them be talking about at this late hour, Kit wondered, when they hadn't spoken to each other in years. He didn't know the exact details, but believed his father and aunt had fallen out after she had altered one of his spells. Wizards are known to be very proud and stubborn when it comes to their magic—witches too for that matter.

Kit slithered out of bed, went to his door and opened it a crack. Was he hoping to hear something this high up in the house? Raised voices perhaps, or smashing ornaments, or flares of magic being fired back and forth as past ill feelings were dredged up? Yet apart from the lazy tick of the old grandfather clock the house remained cold and silent.

Despite everything, Kit suddenly became curious—his curiosity leading him down the stairs, knowing which steps were the creakers to be avoided. By the time he reached the bottom he was much more like his old self.

He paused to listen.

'Yes, they're in the study as I thought,' he muttered, adding a touch more darkly, 'Father thinks he can keep everything from me by shutting me out. That's not fair, I deserve to know more than anyone. After all it was me that caused everything to happen tonight.'

He sounded quite proud of himself, which he wasn't. Anyway not for Henry getting hurt, or his father losing his position at the Palace.

The hallway tiles struck cold against his bare feet. Kit knelt down at the study door, his eye pressed to the keyhole.

Sure enough his aunt and father were together, but there were no raised voices, no shards of broken pottery, and no flashes of orange magic. Kit felt a twinge of disappointment.

'She will see sense eventually,' Aunt Pearl was saying. She was sitting in the same chair that Mr Obb had sat in earlier, her hands wonderfully quick as she knitted.

'I doubt that,' said Dr Stixby glumly. 'I know the Queen and once she gets an idea fixed in her head she's unmovable, and what with that odious man Sparks at her elbow egging her on . . . ' He shook his head. 'I still can't believe it has come to an end. Me, the last in a long line of faithful wizards and witches.'

'You must write the Queen a letter first thing in the morning,' said Aunt Pearl. 'You must explain to her that history can't and mustn't be dismissed so easily, that your magic is worth a thousand little 'lectric boxes. Say that. Make it very clear but respectful, in your best handwriting.'

Dr Stixby was unconvinced.

'Meantime,' continued Aunt Pearl, putting aside her needles and picking up a cup and saucer from the table beside her, 'there remains the problem of that no good nephew of mine.'

'Kit?'

'You know the old saying, Charles—an untamed child makes for untamed magic—and it's true. His magic is as green as a willow wand and will lead him astray if he continues much further along this path. Heavens, Charles, need I remind you, a life was nearly lost tonight.'

'But Kit isn't—'

'He lacks a woman's touch, so important at this stage of his life. Do you know, when I first saw him at the Tower I thought him no better than the other ragamuffins he was running wild with, and certainly no nephew of mine. Have you taken a good look at him recently, Charles? Have you taken enough time away from your magic to do that? His hair is a tangle, his clothes a disgrace, his boots have seen little in the way of spit and polish; and his neck, well . . . I have seen cleaner spades that have spent a whole morning digging up potatoes—'

She went to stir her tea, stopped, and stared down suspiciously. 'Charles—why have you given me a fork with my tea?'

'Eh?' Dr Stixby shifted uncomfortably. 'Mmm . . . there appears to be an unexplained shortage of spoons at the moment.'

Aunt Pearl seized on this at once. 'This is precisely what I mean. There are no rules in the house, Charles. A boy needs consistency.'

'Well I suppose—'

'Something must be done.'

'It could well be—'

'The sooner the better, Charles.'

'It's not that—'

'So you agree to my taking him off your hands for a while, to him coming to live with me . . . To learn a little more self-control?'

Dr Stixby opened his mouth to speak.

'Never in a million years!'

Aunt Pearl stared hard at him. But the anguished cry had not come from Dr Stixby. It had arisen from behind the hallway door.

Chapter Five

Promptly ordered back to bed, Kit lay in a burning fury. It was *so* unfair, no one had even bothered to listen to a single word of what he had to say, in fact the more he protested the more his father seemed to grow convinced that a stay with Aunt Pearl made good sense.

'I'm being kidnapped,' said Kit bubbling with angry magic. And he told his father as much again the following day. 'Besides,' he continued darkly, 'you haven't seen Aunt Pearl in years, you don't know what she's like—what she's really like. She may have changed into summat awful. Anyway I think she's a bit round the twist. Prob'ly she'll send me the same way, *then* you'll be sorry.'

'Don't be silly, Kit,' said Dr Stixby. 'And I won't have you being so rude about your aunt. She'll be here at any moment . . . '

Aunt Pearl arrived at three o'clock on the dot, the grandfather clock chiming the hour. Reluctantly Kit opened the door to her and she thrust her broomstick at him as she swept in.

She removed her gloves and eyed herself in the hallway mirror. Her battered hat met with critical approval.

'Good afternoon, nephew, we mustn't delay, traffic is already quite dreadful. I shall have to write to the authorities. Twice my broom was nearly made into matchsticks by some uniformed madman of a blimp driver.'

Kit spat out a spark of magic and secretly wished the blimps better luck next time. Choosing to ignore his surly silence, Aunt Pearl ran her fingers along the hallway-stand and examined them for dust, although she was embarrassed to be caught doing so when Dr Stixby poked his head around his study door; if nothing else, thought Kit, at least he appeared suitably saddened.

Silently his aunt and father led him up the stairs, their mood so solemn they might have been leading him to the scaffold and not to his bedroom. Carpet lay ready with Kit's packed trunk upon it. Aunt Pearl tutted as her eyes flittered over the rest of the room, taking in the dirty socks and cobwebs. She shot Dr Stixby a this-is-another-example-of-what-I-mean look, at the same time slamming shut several drawers with a casual point of her finger.

Dr Stixby placed a hand on Kit's shoulder.

'I know you think hard of me, Kit, but one day you will see it's for the best.'

Kit shrugged off the hand and refused to look anywhere in his father's direction.

'Are we ready?' asked Aunt Pearl, throwing open the window; and she muttered, 'I do so hate leaving by a window, it appears so common.'

As Kit sat on his trunk waiting to fly into exile, he suddenly remembered something, gave a shout and rushed to the wardrobe. Inside, Hector hung upside down, asleep on his coathanger. He awoke a little bad-temperedly as Kit gently carried him to the window. There was no message in his ring but Henry would understand. Kit kissed the little bat on the head, opened wide his hands and released him into the drab afternoon.

Aunt Pearl did raise a quizzical eyebrow, but without a word of explanation Kit marched back to his trunk and sat down heavily, all joy gone from him once more.

'Take care, Kit,' called his father softly. 'I promise to send a winged letter every day.'

'Come on, Carpet, get a move on,' snapped Kit, and without glancing back he rose and was gone.

It occurred to Kit once they were airborne that he didn't have a clue where his aunt lived. He guessed somewhere quiet and somewhere highly respectable, with equally respectable neighbours; and whenever they approached a particularly large villa surrounded by a neat garden he felt sure that this was bound to be his new prison home for the coming few months. But again and again he was proved wrong and they continued to fly further eastwards.

By the time they reached Fulham, Kit was intensely curious, craning his neck as he sat on his trunk. He couldn't imagine his aunt living anywhere in the sooty, blimp infested centre of London, and yet the East End seemed far too ordinary and unfashionable a place. Finally he could stand it no longer.

'Aunt, have we much further to fly?' he enquired in a roundabout way.

'No,' she replied and infuriatingly left it at that.

'But *where* do you actually live, Aunt?' asked Kit, having done with it and asking straight out.

His aunt, elegantly perched upon her broom, lifted her hand from her hat a moment and pointed. 'There—'

Kit pulled a face. The daft old biddy appeared to have pointed at the largest building in view—old St Paul's Cathedral—which soared sheer of the surrounding sea of roofs like a soot-blackened island.

'You live near St Paul's, Aunt?'

'No, not *near* it at all. On it, boy. On it!'

And Kit was so flabbergasted that he was unable to speak for the rest of the journey.

Despite the many red warning lanterns dotted up its sides, the cathedral's massive square tower lay in darkness at the top. They touched down on the lead roof.

'Home,' sighed Aunt Pearl simply.

She pointed up five glow-balls—an unnecessary waste of power when one would have served their needs, but perhaps that was not the point. Perhaps she wanted to show her nephew all there was to 'home'. He was certainly intrigued—greedy even to see everything at once.

His aunt's house was a very small plain building, built of overlapping timbers with a shingle roof and a stone chimney rising at the back. It had one door and one window; and out in front, pots of herbs and other plants created the illusion of a cottage garden.

The tower's parapet made a boundary wall, and amongst the battlements, pinnacles, and stone ledges were countless bundles of sticks of similar size and appearance. Approaching a few steps nearer, Kit saw that each bundle was in fact a nest, and the many nests together formed a single crow colony, the birds flying up in an alarming clatter even as he realized, mobbing Aunt Pearl and cawing harshly.

'Now less of your nonsense,' she said sounding amused. 'It's only my no-good nephew, you must get used to seeing him . . . No—no, of course he isn't interested in taking your eggs.'

Amongst the swirl of wings and feathers, some birds managed to perch on her hat, knocking it more crooked, while others found crowded claw space on her shoulders; however, the greatest number circled above in a black whirlpool, raising such a noise that Kit was equally alarmed and excited by it.

'Will they come to me d'you think?' he asked eagerly.

'Why don't you try,' she answered. 'They will come if they trust you.'

Kit held out his hand and called to the crows encouragingly . . . but after several minutes not one had come near. Kit sulkily thrust his hand back into his pocket. 'Didn't really want one—could magic up my own bird if I did. A better bird—an eagle. A *crow* eating eagle,' he added darkly.

Aunt Pearl swept the sitting birds off her like crumbs and sighed. 'Ah, you have a lot to learn, nephew . . . Now step indoors and be sure to wipe your feet.'

Inside, Kit found the little house just as peculiar as the outside, or as peculiar as the outside promised it would be. A single downstairs room was crammed to the last inch with over-stuffed chairs, sideboards and tables, every possible surface covered in lace doilies, glass-bead mats, and antimacassars; all hung with heavy fringes, tassels or black feathers. And then there were the hosts of knick-knacks—vases, porcelain figures and clocks; with one shelf entirely given over to Aunt Pearl's collection of china crows. No less common were the silver-framed photographs of family wizards and witches, amongst which Kit was surprised to see a family group made up of his mother, his father (as a handsome much younger man), and himself as a tiny baby held lovingly in his mother's arms.

Seeing him stare at it, Aunt Pearl picked it up and sniffed. 'Ah, if only your dear, sweet mother was alive today, things would not be as they are.'

Mainly to change the subject Kit asked, 'Where do *I* sleep?' For he saw a ladder at the side of the room leading to a platform beneath the roof, with room enough on the platform for one very large brass bed, and he didn't suppose for a minute his aunt would want to share that with him, however wide the mattress.

'Why, here will do nicely,' she said, showing him how soft and comfortable the nearest sofa was by prodding one of its cushions. Kit stared at her in disbelief. Wasn't it bad enough not having a room of his own, but to go without a proper bed . . . the notion made him laugh out loud.

That was only the beginning. Kit learned fast just how different life with Aunt Pearl was going to be. For a start she had no cook or maid, and she strongly approved of order and hated mess, forcing Kit to rethink his sloppy old ways of doing things.

With no room inside, supper that night was cooked in the open in an old-fashioned witch's cauldron above a great leaping fire. Aunt Pearl took charge but fully expected Kit to help—and he did, chopping and stirring and fetching for his aunt and returning sharpish for more if she barked at him again. The only thing he didn't do was gather firewood because this was a task done by the crows.

In a grudging way Kit supposed he enjoyed helping, and his aunt's stew and dumplings were well worth the effort, seeming to taste so much nicer when eaten by the fireside—the twigs crackling and sparks flying up through the heat haze into the cold starry London sky.

Supper finished, Aunt Pearl dozed in her armchair and Kit stretched out on Carpet staring deep into the flames; both had eaten well and now were too full to move. Only the crows busied themselves, forever tidying the piles of firewood with their beaks, as if it were as important to them as building a good strong nest. Happening to glance up, Kit suddenly realized that Aunt Pearl wasn't really dozing after all, although it looked that way. He saw her studying him through half closed eyes.

He sat up on Carpet. 'Aunt Pearl,' he said. 'Has there always been a witch living above St Paul's?'

The old woman didn't open her eyes. 'A witch or a wizard.'

'But why?'

'Why-why-why. Why are you so ignorant, boy? Doesn't your father send you to school?'

'Oh, he sends me all right,' admitted Kit. 'Only . . . sometimes . . . I don't seem to arrive.'

'Then listen well to me, nephew, and I will tell you a story.' Her sleepy look gone, Aunt Pearl hung a glow-ball by the side of her head, casting a mysterious light across her face. Kit hugged his knees, paying her his fullest attention—he enjoyed hearing stories.

Aunt Pearl began to tell hers.

'Long ago, when London was much smaller and all its houses were wooden and crowded together, there lived a baker by the name of Thomas Farryner. Now Thomas was a good enough baker in his way, with his own shop in Pudding Lane, but he was a lazy man who hated getting up in the mornings; and like many lazy men before and since, he thought he would solve his problem with a slice of magic. So he paid a visit to a wizard called Septimus Troon who ran a spell shop nearby. Thomas told him his problem and for sixpence the wizard duly sold him a jar of inflamers, one of which, each morning, would light the baker's ovens for him, giving him an extra hour in bed. But the real price of the magic nearly turned out to be the destruction of London.'

'Why, what happened?' whispered Kit.

'For a long time nothing,' continued his aunt. 'Everything went well, just as Thomas wanted and Septimus had promised. The trouble arose because inflamers have a particular smell—'

'I know! It's lovely 'n' sweet like honey.'

56

'—And rats, as well as small boys who interrupt their aunts, find it irresistible.'

'Sorry,' said Kit.

Aunt Pearl frowned.

'Of course Thomas had been warned about this and kept his enchantments on a high shelf. But a rat— especially a hungry one—would have found no difficulty in climbing up and reaching it—and one did, reach it that is. After that it required no more than a clumsy paw or a careless tail to knock over the jar and set it rolling along the shelf, before it fell and smashed on the floor . . . and burst into flames.'

So saying, Aunt Pearl raised an unseen hand, touched the glow-ball and it became a fiery sphere.

Kit jumped with surprise.

'Soon the entire baker's shop was alight—flames flickered from its windows, smoke rose through its thatch. Thomas came running, but by then it was too late—oh, much too late—his shop was no more, and now it was his neighbours' homes and shops that were bright with fire—and the fire spread until all of Pudding Lane was ablaze.'

She clicked her fingers and the hovering flames leapt up with an angry roar. Kit was so thrilled that his skin turned goose-pimply.

'The fire spread out of control to other streets and yet others. It burned houses and shops, warehouses and churches, and still the flames were hungry for more as they moved towards their greatest prize—the old cathedral, to St Paul's itself. The king, safe at Hampton Court, sent for his eight finest wizards and witches and ordered them to save the building at all costs; after all, he told them, a cathedral is the heart of a city and without a heart it is dead. At once the enchanters took their leave and raced straight to London on their broomsticks, seeing it first as a red glow in the night: amongst the eight were the great alchemist Juno, and Gruffydd the discoverer of perpetual motion, and Orlando, called by many *Lord of Ghosts* because he was served by things invisible.

'They arrived just in time, the flames were about to throw themselves forwards and take hold of St Paul's' ancient stones. Quickly the eight enchanters placed themselves in the path of the fire and each called up a cloud, and each filled his or her cloud with as much water as it would hold. When full, the rains began to fall fast and heavy—with flashes of lightning and magic, and long terrible rolls of thunder. Caught between rain and flames, the enchanters stood firm, although the fire sizzled with fury; it scorched the walls and melted the roof and shattered the glass, but it did not get inside. The old cathedral stood much as it stands today, even though all of the houses around it were gone, every one of them burned to a mound of ash . . . And that, my no-good nephew, is what happened during what later became known as the Great Fire of London.'

With the ending of the tale, Aunt Pearl's flaming glow-ball died down abruptly and once more became smooth and pale and creamy—like a shining peach.

'So the cathedral was saved?' said Kit breathing out his words admiringly.

'Badly damaged, but yes, it was saved,' replied Aunt Pearl. 'Afterwards some tried to argue that it should still be pulled down and be replaced by a fancy new building with a huge dome instead of a tower. Mercifully nothing ever came of the plan—just as well, I should hate to live on a dome. Absolutely no privacy at all and I should keep thinking I was going to fall off.'

'Was the king pleased?'

'The king . . . ? Extremely. And as a special honour he promised each enchanter a monument to be remembered by, and they all chose the same thing, do you know what?'

Kit shook his head.

'A gargoyle.'

'A gargoyle?' repeated Kit.

'You *do* know what a gargoyle is, don't you, boy?'

Kit shrugged. 'A kind of statue thing up on the roof—that's it, like a monster, isn't it? And when it rains it looks a bit like they're spitting at you—though I reckon none can spit as good as my pal Alfie Tanner can.'

'*Spit*—heavens above, boy.' His aunt sounded horrified. 'Well bred gargoyles never spit, they spout with the elegance of a Meissen teapot. Only common little church gargoyles *spit*.'

'And do the gargoyles have names?' asked Kit hurriedly.

'Indeed they do. The same names as their masters and mistresses. Let me see, starting from the east there's Philemon, Balthasar, Juno, Xerxes, Mignon, Orlando, Gotheric, and Gruffydd. And apart from spouting beautifully they stand watch over the cathedral like lions, protecting it from its enemies.'

Kit nodded his head in satisfaction. 'That's a good story, Aunt, you told it well. I'd prob'ly go to school more often if lessons were as good as yours.' He picked up a twig from the edge of the fire. 'You know, in a way it reminds me of Henry. He always used to tell me stories about his family and all his different ancestors; of course being a royal it amounted to the same thing as a history lesson, but it was *really* int'resting because you could actually see them as proper living people.'

'Ah, Henry,' said Aunt Pearl softly. 'I sense he troubles your thoughts even though we speak of different matters.'

Kit looked up and scowled. 'Wouldn't be my friend if he didn't.'

'Quite so. And I'm afraid I have no news to give you as to his present well-being. I flew to the Palace first thing this morning but was sent away rather sharpishly without finding out a thing. If you like, though, I can send a goodwill spell and hope it cheers him up.'

Kit smiled. 'Yes, Henry would like that . . . thank you.' He brightened suddenly. 'And in the morning will you show me the gargoyles and tell me all their names again so I can remember? Then I will be able to tell Henry about them next time I see him. Oh, and you still haven't answered my original question. Why do *you* live on the tower?'

'Can't you guess?' Aunt Pearl smiled coyly. 'I am the gargoyles' mistress, they obey me as loyally as a pack of hounds. Without a witch or wizard in control, how are they to recognize a friend from an enemy? And you needn't wait till morning to see them. They are behind you as I speak.'

Kit's head jerked around as if he had been given a hefty punch on the chin. He gasped at what he saw then clutched at his aunt's skirts.

'You haven't listened to me at all,' she said sharply. 'You won't come to any harm unless I wish it and give the command.'

'Tell 'em to keep away. Tell 'em!' croaked Kit.

Aunt Pearl smiled. 'Foolish boy, they are only curious.'

Kit forced himself to look again. The gargoyles had crawled closer. He saw fangs and claws and folded wings; and eyes that bulged and tails that dragged heavily along the ground like spiked weapons of war. They were so hideous he found himself laughing nervously with horror.

But Aunt Pearl stretched down and stroked them as she would a dog, as one by one they came up to her—her fingers running over humps and spines and twisted horns.

Then Kit knew he simply had to touch one. Gingerly he reached out his hand, his fingertips brushing a tail. A gargoyle turned and two intelligent eyes peered at him down a long crocodile-like snout. Slowly the creature approached and stood before him, waiting to be petted properly. Kit forced out his hand, ready to snatch it back at any moment. He touched the gargoyle a second time, briefly stroking its ear, then pulled away his hand in any case.

'Balthasar enjoys having his ears tickled,' said Aunt Pearl, 'especially at the back where the moss grows that he can't reach with his claws.'

So Kit reached out his hand again and tickled the gargoyle's mossy ears until Balthasar closed his eyes in sheer pleasure.

Kit laughed out loud. Then he couldn't be content until he had stroked every one of the eight gargoyles. Some were soft, some scaly, some had feathers and some hard leathery skins.

'Enough now,' said Aunt Pearl presently. 'It's been a busy day, boy, and already way past your bedtime.'

Kit looked at her astonished. 'But, Aunt, I don't ever go to bed *this* early, it wouldn't be right. My magic doesn't reach its strongest until midnight and . . . Ah, but perhaps you don't know much about boys and how we are, not having had someone my age stay with you before. Actually,' he said with a swagger, 'I never go to bed much before moon-down.'

'At Richmond perhaps,' replied his aunt. 'But here things are different. To start with I want to see your face and neck pink and gleaming. A good scrub will tire you out, boy, if you do it properly.'

'Oh no—not me,' cried Kit jumping up. 'I'm not a baby. You can't make me do anything I don't want!'

Aunt Pearl rose wearily and began to limp back to her

house, followed by her faithful chair. 'No—you're quite right, boy, *I* can't make you. But . . . hum . . . my gargoyles can.'

As she passed through her doorway, Kit felt something tug at his leg. He looked down to see Balthasar had seized it in his jaws. Then Philemon wrapped his long clawed feet around Kit's other leg and was trying to climb up it; and all the other gargoyles were crowding around.

'Aunt! Aunt!' screamed Kit.

He heard her chuckle as he fell backwards onto the roof. The next moment the gargoyles were on top of him, holding him down and giving him a thorough washing with their long, wet slimy tongues.

How Kit howled.

How he struggled.

How he wished he had used soap and water when he had the chance.

But there was no escape until the gargoyles were done, by which time he was sopping wet from head to foot and twice as dejected.

'And don't drip on my carpet,' ordered Aunt Pearl waiting for him by the door.

Chapter Six

After a few days Kit decided that living with Aunt Pearl was rather like living with two completely different people. First there was the crazy old witch lady who shared her life with crows and gargoyles; who rode off on her broomstick at four o'clock in the morning to find toadstools; who collected dead pieces of hide and feathers and made use of them in her magic—and even owned a royal warrant, permitting her to visit the Queen's menagerie at the Tower for that very purpose.

Second, there was the extremely proper matronly aunt, who took tea in her best china whenever her witch lady friends called; who spent most of her day making spells and potions for the free magic hospital at St Bartholomew's; who was fond of saying, 'A home for everything not in use'; and whose doormat was trained to grab the heels of anyone who did not wipe his feet properly (as Kit discovered!).

Aunt Pearl was a stickler for rules and routines and these made no allowance for half wild, grubby little boys; she expected Kit to help her with the housework in the morning and with her magic in the afternoon; and until she could trust him to stay out of mischief he was not allowed to go a single step beyond the cathedral. Sometimes that felt quite odd to Kit: gazing down on all London while not being a part of it.

To keep it that way, Aunt Pearl locked a weight spell on to Carpet, making it too heavy to fly, and from her eight devoted gargoyles she appointed Balthasar to be Kit's special guardian to keep watch over him at all times, especially if she happened to be away collecting ingredients for her magic.

'Balthasar, see that my no-good nephew does not burn down the cathedral in my absence,' she would say, fixing her hat; and Balthasar would grin with a mouth wide enough to spout rainwater as elegantly as a Meissen teapot and wink a fond eye at Kit. Out of all the gargoyles he was the most playful and affectionate, despite his fierce weathered appearance.

And then there was Sinclair M. Pickerdoon . . .

Sinclair M. Pickerdoon was an old, dear friend of Aunt Pearl's and a Shakespearean wizard by training. He wore yellow tartan trousers three inches too short for him and was quite the worst broomstick rider that Kit had ever seen, managing on three separate visits to strike the cathedral's parapet, the flagpole, and Aunt Pearl's chimney stack. He came so frequently because of Aunt Pearl's determined belief that Kit needed an education and, while he was between acting jobs, Mr Pickerdoon was the right man to give him one.

At first Mr Pickerdoon was appalled by Kit's lack of knowledge in algebra and geography, but glowed with pleasure at his magical abilities.

'He points di-vinely,' he would coo, with exaggerated sweeps of his hand, tilts of his head, and such dramatic movements of his eyes, mouth, and eyebrows that Kit always had to stop himself from laughing. In a voice deep and sonorous, Mr Pickerdoon spoke to Kit as if Kit were his audience, and elaborately rolled his r's off his tongue so that anything he said took an age to finish.

Whenever feeling particularly lazy, Kit knew just the smallest mention of his tutor's hero was enough to sidetrack him and put an end to any work.

'Did Shakespeare like doing 'rithmatic, Mr Pickerdoon?'

Or—

'Suppose Shakespeare knew a lot more about history than me on account of him living much closer to it.'

That was all it required, and when all else failed there was always Mr Pickerdoon's time as a Shakespearean actor to fall back on.

'Oh, dearrrrr boy, you have no idea, I may be a thirrrrrd rrrrrate actorrrrr, but as a wizarrrrrd you should see my special effects. They still rrrrremarrrrrk upon my blasted heath rrrrright to this verrrrry day.'

Between his aunt and Mr Pickerdoon, Kit was kept so busy that it was only at night, when the fire crackled low and with the gargoyles curled at his feet and everything slowing down to sleep, that he was able to think about his friend Henry and wonder how he was. Worryingly there had been no news from the Palace despite Aunt Pearl's frequent calls there—all they knew for sure was that Stafford Sparks had taken absolute control and anything slightly touched by magic was turned away at the gate.

Then one night Hector reappeared, fluttering down out of the darkness and suddenly latching spread-eagled onto Kit's chest. Although greatly surprised, Kit managed to keep it silent; and a quick glance in his aunt's direction told him that she had been too preoccupied with her knitting to notice anything out of the usual. Only watchful old Balthasar saw, tilting his head with curiosity.

Kit hurriedly unpicked Hector from the front of his coat: poor thing must have travelled miles to find him and was quite worn out. Kit slipped him into the warmth of his pocket and made an excuse to go into his aunt's house. Once safely out of sight he took out the little bat, who had fallen asleep, and found the message tied to his leg. Kit's fingers trembled. Clumsily he undid the letter and started to read.

Oh, Kit, help me, I believe Mr Sparks and his
electric shock treatment are doing more harm than
good, but nobody listens when I say so—they just
keep telling me that Sparks is a genius. Even
Grandmama thinks so. But I cannot stand the man
near me, he makes my flesh crawl, and I think he
enjoys hurting me with that horrible electric box of
his.

> *Please say you'll help.*
> *As ever, your best friend*
> *H*

Kit read the letter with a deep and growing sense of anger; if only Stafford Sparks knew it, he was already his greatest enemy, and if necessary Kit would go and shout it in his face. But first, Henry needed him. Stuffing the letter into his pocket and leaving Hector to sleep from a hook in the wall, Kit went out to his aunt. Balthasar stared at him with amusement, but Kit was in no mood for the gargoyle's sly little games.

'Aunt Pearl,' said Kit trying to control his shaky voice.

'Umm . . .' She had dropped a stitch and was busily counting those that remained.

'Aunt Pearl, suppose it was me that was bit by a werewolf. You know, not Henry but me. What would you have done to cure me? I only ask because I'm int'rested and think it's educational to know—in case it happens again. And it might, specially now—what with werewolves in London and all that.'

Kit hoped he didn't sound too obvious, and wished Balthasar would stop staring at him as if reading him like a page of trouble. Aunt Pearl looked up.

'Werewolf's bite . . . Let me see . . .' She thrust the needles through the ball of wool. 'If it's a fresh bite then you need little more than a straightforward lotion: berry

66

juice from a churchyard yew, mixed with ten death-watch beetles—dried and ground; garlic, as you'd expect and as much as possible; some dried skin from a cobra and a spoonful or so of sneezewort against fever. Oh, and not forgetting a nice hungry leech about a week later to draw out any remaining poison.'

'And if it is an old wound?'

'More difficult.' Aunt Pearl paused to think. 'Garlic again, of course, but you would need other, stronger ingredients: dragon's bile, poison from a cockatrice, and several dried salamanders crushed into a fine powder.'

Kit already knew the exact place in his aunt's poison cabinet where she kept the dragon's bile and dried salamanders. 'Er, I expect cockatrice poison is so rare that you don't have none?' he remarked innocently.

'Indeed I do,' replied Aunt Pearl proudly. 'Milked it myself. It's on the top shelf of the poisons, in a little blue glass bottle with a stopper like a silver star.'

Kit had found out all he wished to know. He smiled across at Balthasar as if to say, 'Look how clever I am.'

Balthasar's eyes remained wide and watchful.

Kit was far too fretful to sleep well that night and lay on the sofa listening to his aunt's snores. He had been dying to ask her when she would be next away from the tower, but such a question might appear *too* conspicuous and raise his aunt's suspicions. To his great relief, however, early the following morning he saw her put on her hat and stand in front of the mirror, trying to get the wilted flowers to remain upright. As usual she soon lost patience with them and they drooped back down again in disarray.

'Are you going out, Aunt?' asked Kit, mildly interested.

'Yes,' she snapped, 'so you needn't stand idly by. If you've nothing better to do go get out your books ready for when Mr Pickerdoon arrives.'

Ah yes, Mr Pickerdoon. Kit smiled to himself.

Still in a temper over her hat, Aunt Pearl shouted for her broom.

'Watch out for blimps,' said Kit as pleasantly as could be.

'Hmph.'

He watched her fly up into the sky and a few minutes later saw another broomstick come into view, approaching from a different direction, and he instantly recognized the rider's yellow tartan trousers. Mr Pickerdoon headed directly at the tower, rose violently at the last moment and crashed down onto the roof.

'Mr Pickerdoon—Mr Pickerdoon! Are you all right, sir? Have you broken both legs or is it just one of 'em?' Kit rushed up to the old actor showing great concern. Mr Pickerdoon leapt up beaming and took a bow.

'Ahhhhh, dearrrrr boy, yourrrrr fearrrrrrs arrrrre most touching . . . but com-pletely un-necessarrrrrry.'

'You look a bit peaky, Mr Pickerdoon. Let me help you into the house—that's right, lean on me. You sure you're not bleeding nowhere?'

In the short time it took Kit to help him into the house and onto a sofa, he managed to persuade Mr Pickerdoon that he might well be seriously injured after all; and Mr Pickerdoon soon played a willing part with drooping expression and a limp hand pressed to his forehead.

'I best make you a cup of tea,' said Kit. 'Tea and lots of sugar are good for shock.'

'Yes—the tea, dearrrrr boy, and *do* please hurrrrry.'

Kit grinned. That was easy—as easy as dropping a strong sleeping spell into a teacup; Kit prayed it didn't curdle the milk.

Mr Pickerdoon seized the dainty cup and saucer from him as soon as he reappeared. It might have been vital medicine, while he might have been the dying man who needed it, to judge from the performance he gave, gulping down the tea in one. Instantly he fell into a sleep so deep that Kit had to prise the cup from his fingers, raised halfway to his mouth.

Now Kit knew he must work fast. He raided his aunt's poison cabinet and snatched down a mixing-bowl. Soon he had the right ingredients set out before him, but the trouble was he was unsure about each one's measure; for good or bad he would have to follow his own magical instincts.

He took a breath. 'Here goes,' he said.

He dripped half the brown treacly dragon's bile into the bowl, added salamander powder and three drops of sparkling cockatrice venom, stirring them together with a few muttered charms. The mixture bubbled and smoked, filling the air with an evil smell. As he slept, wisps of the smoke drifted past Mr Pickerdoon's twitching nostrils and he called out in alarm:

'Angels and ministerrrrrs of grrrrrace defend us!

Be thou a spirrrrrit of health or goblin damned.'

'Oh, hush up with that ol' Shakespeare stuff!' cried Kit irritably. He mixed the lotion thoroughly and carefully poured it into an empty bottle, then tied down the stopper with string and thrust it deep into his pocket. Mr Pickerdoon was snoring contentedly as Kit slipped through the door and quietly closed it behind him.

'Oh—Balthasar.'

The moment Kit turned around, the gargoyle was there in front of him. He raised a single quizzical eyebrow and grinned, revealing between his fangs a stone ball taken from the top of one of the cathedral's pinnacles. He wanted to play the game they had invented—in it Kit struggled to roll the heavy stone along the roof, while Balthasar would retrieve it without the slightest difficulty. The game was all to do with strength and amused the gargoyle immensely—Kit too. Usually . . .

'Not now, Balthasar, eh. Mr Pickerdoon has just told me to go down into the cathedral and study some int'resting inscriptions—in Latin I shouldn't wonder. Shan't be long—you needn't trouble yourself to come with me.' Although he knew Balthasar would.

Without brooms and carpets to rely on, the only way down from the tower was by dark, twisting stairway. This led first to a gallery overlooking the cathedral's great bells which shone dully in the light of Kit's glow-ball, but were mostly covered in cobwebs and bats' droppings, having never been used in years because the cathedral was no longer considered safe enough to ring them. Then the mean twisting stairway continued on, and Kit who followed it down was not at all happy at having to go so slowly, mindful of each and every treacherous step; and he was even less happy when he caught the distinct thump-thump-thump of Balthasar's tail as the gargoyle followed distantly behind.

Finally Kit reached a small door at the bottom. Blowing out his glow-ball he stepped out into the main part of the cathedral, carefully latching the door behind him (at best it might delay Balthasar by a few minutes). This done he slipped across to a stone column which felt cold against his cheek and was so fat that his arms could not stretch halfway around it. Well hidden here, he peered out into the cathedral's dark, gloomy nave, seeing only one other person and this was the bishop himself, a small, crooked, sour faced man hurrying by.

As he drew level with Kit he stopped to cough, causing a trail of stone dust to fall upon his bald head from the high vaulted ceiling. Bad temperedly he brushed it off, pulled his purple cloak tightly about him, then proceeded towards the high altar, his feet clip-clopping upon the cold, worn flagstones.

Kit shadowed him noiselessly, first dodging from one pillar to the next as if through a forest of stone trees, then crawling along behind the wooden choir stalls.

Suddenly the bishop stopped, glaring back flinty eyed towards the nave. Somewhere some fool was banging on a door—Kit held his breath knowing it to be Balthasar.

'Confounded racket,' scowled the bishop. In the high, grey shafts of light, trickles of stone dust cascaded from various parts of the old building, and Kit felt the gritty dust beneath his hands where he crouched.

The bishop again pulled his heavy cloak about him, and Kit noticed that the cold had turned his nose almost the same shade of purple, the drip at the end like a gleaming pearl. Leaving the persistent noise for one of his underlings to deal with, the bishop turned and clip-clopped away and was soon gone.

Alone at last, Kit ran to the door that led to the crypt. He bolted through it and down a short flight of steps. Below ground the damp, creeping darkness slowed him to a skulk, and felt thick enough to rub between his thumb and finger as when a tailor sizes-up cloth.

'Glow-ball—where are you?' he whispered anxiously, for the absolute dark frightened him more than he cared to admit.

Slowly a glow-ball lifted from the stone slab top of a nearby tomb, like something rising from its grave to haunt him.

'This is no time for larking about,' said Kit sharply. He shivered and stroked his arms. 'Not here, not in this creepy hole and see you don't shine so brightly either, I don't want Balthasar spotting mc the minute he arrives because you're beaming on me like a spotlight.'

The glow-ball floated up to the crypt's low ceiling like a balloon, casting dim, ghostly light onto crowded rows of monuments, some with faded coats of arms, others with rotting flags or broken effigies. Kit didn't like what was revealed one little bit, deciding this place was best left to the dead; and it seemed everywhere he turned there were skulls—either carved ones, or real ones set in niches in the walls, grinning gap-toothed at him, each sitting on top of a jigsaw puzzle heap of ancient bones.

'Bah—they're only scraps of old people anyway,' scoffed Kit, who knew he had to overcome his fears and concentrate on his powers. Wizard instincts had told him on previous explorations of the cathedral that a secret passage was here somewhere, only where exactly was for him to find out. But how he wished he had bothered to look for it before when he had the chance to take time over it and do the job properly.

Closing his eyes he sent his mind out walking . . . It went through the empty eye sockets of many hollow heads without touching anything; and all the time it wanted to come back home because it was afraid.

Then at the door at the top of the steps something began to scratch and burrow at the wood—a gargoyle claw perhaps?

Kit urged his mind further on, sending it crawling along the walls until it found a crack and pushed its way in. He had no idea where he was, he needed another living mind to tell him that. Then by sheer good fortune he found one, walking straight into the head of an unsuspecting graveyard rat.

It was a simple mind of course, at first unaware of its visitor.

Hungry-hungry-hungry. *Eat-eat-eat*. *Hungry-hungry-hungry*. *Eat-eat-eat*. So ran the rat's only thoughts just then until—

Hello, said Kit.

Ekk! Something there! Something there? Yes. Well eat it if small, run away from it if big. Wait, wait . . . no smell . . . no sound . . . no see. Ekk! Danger-danger-danger.

I won't harm you, promised Kit. *I just want to know summat. Listen, I need a way out of here—a secret passage, if you happen to know of one.*

Secret passage? said the rat timidly.

Hole . . . burrow, explained Kit, using terms with which he thought the rat might be more familiar. *A burrow big enough for a boy . . . a man-pup.*

Immediately Kit sensed terror. *You—man? A meatless man with nothing left to gnaw on?*

Meatless man? Oh, I'm not a skeleton, if that's what you mean. I'm as much living and breathing as you are, but I need your help.

You want Rat help? There was an uneasy pause then— *Maggots on your stinking body!* Kit jumped at the violence of the rat's curse. *You boys kill rats with stones. Huh, now you expect Rat to help you?*

Yes—oh please—look, I'm sorry if some boys do kill your people, said Kit desperately. *I never have—or will; and I'll give you half a biscuit if you help me—food, Rat.*

Fo-od! Hungry-hungry-hungry . . . Oh why you not say so first? Rat—he agree.

Good, I somehow thought you might. Now come out and let me see you.

First promise no tricks or traps—not be like that boy who got my rat-lations in Hamelin. You say the promise.

I promise.

Hey—then what that big bang crash noise?

Oh no, it's Balthasar. I have to get away. Quickly show me, Rat, and the biscuit is yours.

Kit called back his mind and it returned so forcibly that his eyes suddenly jerked open. He saw his new rat friend (to be honest a rather small, brown, scrawny individual) already waiting for him on a crumbling tomb, sitting up on his back legs, whiskers twitching. Then both boy and rat turned in dismay hearing Balthasar's powerful blows against the door. The gargoyle would be through it at any moment and the crypt was high enough for him to stretch his wings and fly. It would be the easiest thing in the world for him to swoop down and pounce on Kit like a great lithe cat.

Rat set off, leaping from tomb to tomb, while Kit was forced to squeeze his way between them, grazing his legs and hands in the process. Then Rat scrambled over the stone face of a past Lord Mayor and sprang onto one of the strangest monuments Kit had ever set eyes on. It was exactly like a ticket booth, with a bust of the man it commemorated set behind the counter like a ticket clerk— and he was laughing.

Underneath were carved these words:

Daniel Trywitt 1744–1812
'May his ticket to Heaven be one way.' A man of many
noble qualities and achievements: not least amongst the
last was his building of the city's very first
UNDERGROUND RAILWAY; which led to the discovery
of the lost tribes of London—the BURROW PEOPLE. A
good husband, fine father, worthy friend, notable
engineer and the most insufferable PRACTICAL JOKER in
all of England.

Rat ran excitedly around the base of this odd looking structure.

'It's no use,' wailed Kit. '*You* may be able to squeeze through those tiny chinks and cracks at the bottom, but I can't.'

In desperation he tried to shift the monument with his

bare hands, hearing all the while the cracking of door-wood and half expecting at any minute Balthasar's jaws to close upon his collar, dragging him back to the tower.

'. . . . most insufferable practical joker in all of England.'

For some reason, again more to do with wizardly intuition than anything else, these words seemed to spring up and catch Kit's eye, and with them came the craziest idea. Taking a penny from his pocket he pushed it into the slot on the counter. He heard it drop, striking against metal, and the stone head of Daniel Trywitt nodded mechanically; after which all manner of things happened: cogs turned, stone ground upon stone, and the monument smoothly slid back revealing steps.

'It's worked!' cried Kit amazed.

Without a second thought he hurtled down the steps, only remembering at the last moment to fling Rat his reward. Rat vanished at once, and Kit pulled a lever and the monument slid back into place overhead; as it did so Balthasar flew at it screaming in fury and scoring his claws down the stonework. Yet for all his terrifying noise the monument was simply too solid for him to smash.

'Sorry, Balthasar,' whispered Kit, genuinely regretful at having tricked the gargoyle for whom he had developed a real affection. Still, his escape had been a close thing and now Kit's legs shook so badly that he needed to sit down in the dark for a full five minutes before he was ready to go on. When able to point without his hand shaking he called up a glow-ball and followed it down some steps and along a passage, not knowing where it was taking him but hoping to arrive at some place useful.

And he did.

At another ticket office in fact, a proper one this time, at St Paul's Underground Station, emerging through a door marked 'Private. Mr Trywitt's living room'.

Kit grimaced at the feebleness of the joke and looked around worried in case he was greeted by the hostile stares of clerks or the questioning looks of passengers as they queued up to buy their tickets, but this did not happen. The station was unlit and spookily deserted; old tickets scattered along the platform like autumn leaves.

Then Kit noticed that the advertisements and information boards were covered in posters and the posters all said the same thing:

Closed for rebuilding work
By order
Stafford Sparks
(Superintendent of Scientific Progress)

Kit furiously seized one and tore it down.

Chapter Seven

From the deserted underground station Kit made his way up the main passenger stairs; meeting on the way more than one set of chained and locked gates—yet these proved no match against an angry blast of magic, flying apart in a shower of blue and white sparks. Then reaching street level he slipped unnoticed out of the station, feeling greatly relieved to be back amongst the dirt, noise, and bustle of London once more.

He guessed it to be about mid-day, but it was difficult to be sure since the dreary light made it seem much later, not helped by the rain which had begun to fall steadily onto hats and bonnets and black umbrellas. The wet pavements were unusually crowded, people pushing their way along; Kit pushed with them and more than once somebody turned and snarled: 'Watch where you're going, boy.' Then a nanny drove her mechanical perambulator straight through the middle of the throng, and two tiny infants peered out at Kit, snug beneath its raised hood— like twin pearls in an oyster shell.

'*Do* mind your backs, please,' called the nanny from her high driving seat at the rear; her raincoat was buttoned up tightly to her neck and glistened with rain, and she honked a big brass horn.

Kit dodged into a shop doorway as the perambulator spluttered past in a cloud of kerosene; and the moment it was gone the crowds surged back filling the space where it had been.

'This push and shove is thoroughly ridiculous,' said a

large woman in a cape like an unpegged tent, turning to her friend. 'That fellow Sparks has over-reached himself this time. Imagine closing most of the Central Line and for what? To make it all electric. Huh, the man has a positive mania for electricity.'

'Quite,' agreed her friend, freeing her shopping basket with an ungainly tug. 'And what was wrong with the old steam trains in the first place? My doctor says that coal smoke happens to be very good for you—cleans your lungs . . .'

The two women were swept along, replaced by new voices complaining about the closure of the Underground. Kit only half listened, drawn by the name of his sworn enemy, Stafford Sparks. He stood deep in thought staring over the roof-tops and telegraph lines to St Paul's, blackened by centuries of soot and rising so high that its tower snagged the ragged grey rain clouds. Even from a distance Kit clearly recognized Gotheric, Gruffydd, and Philemon, now as much stone as the walls they gripped; and his aunt was right, they *did* spout beautifully. Kit thought he must make a point of telling them if ever he met the gargoyles again . . . and if Balthasar had forgiven him enough to listen.

'Poor Balthasar.'

Again Kit felt desperately sorry for having tricked the gargoyle; but it had to be done, Henry was in trouble and Kit would have risked far more to go to the help of his friend.

Remembering Henry, Kit plunged back into the crowds and fought his way along Newgate Street. Overhead, the iron gantries thronged with people waiting to catch a blimp, their umbrellas jammed together and forming an almost complete roof; and on the road the traffic was heavy and slow, tooting and hissing impatiently: an endless line of motorized pennyfarthings, sparking trams, and steam carriages like fat smoking pumpkins. A cavalry officer on a turbine horse flashed its eye-like headlamps at Kit for daring to step off the pavement in front of him, then purposely splashed Kit as he went by. And there, like something from another age, was an old-fashioned horse-drawn carriage, ridden in by a quaint, grey-haired couple who, decided Kit, were probably down from the country since they looked utterly lost and uncomfortable in the big city. This being so, their footman had all his necessary wits about him, and when a brewer's steam-dray gave out a dirty puff of soot sending the horses rearing in terror, he dashed forward and managed to calm them.

The pavement came to a complete standstill as idle onlookers stopped to gawp as if at something quite remarkable; while a pompous little red-faced man took it upon himself to speak what many around him must have been thinking.

'It makes no sense,' he said. 'Horses on the roads of central London are a ruddy menace these days. Ought to have a law against it. Absolutely shocking.'

Some nodded in agreement, although his words hung heavy on Kit. Was it because magic, like horses and carriages, was becoming a thing of the past? Unreasonably angry he turned round meaning to knock the little red-faced man's hat into the gutter with a sly jab of magic, but instead he instantly forgot all thoughts of revenge and his whole expression lit up.

He had spied a familiar face.

'Hey, Tommy!' he bellowed above the hissing air-brakes of an arriving blimp.

Across the road his friend was sitting on a small crooked building between two much taller and more imposing ones, which were usefully keeping most of the rain off him. He sat on a parapet above a large clock, swinging his legs; and he gave the impression of being

bored, both of his own company and with his magic—
despite the pigeons around him glowing every colour
imaginable and the hands of the clock ticking
backwards.

Kit was forced to shout a good few times before Tommy
eventually heard and looked down. Seeing Kit, he grinned
with delight.

'Kit! Hey, what's up—you haven't lost Carpet, have
you? Ha-ha. You look like some old beggar-wizard down
there. Ain't you got nothing to ride on?'

'It's a long story,' shouted Kit. 'Give us a lift, eh,
Tommy.'

With a whoop, Tommy leapt off the parapet and threw
his leg over his broom like a bronco rider, even as he fell
with it. Then taking control he swept low over the heads
of the crowds, hovered a few seconds to give Kit time to
reach up and get a firm hold of the handle, then lifted him
up and clean away, taking him back to his roof. The
multicoloured pigeons flew away in fright.

'Well,' beamed Tommy, 'I'm not doing much else at
the moment, what's this here long story of yours? I'm in
need of a spot of cheering up at present.'

'Oh, it's nothing really,' said Kit suddenly embarrassed.
'Only my Aunt Pearl's gone and bewitched Carpet and
she says she won't lift the spell until she thinks I deserve
it. Huh, at this rate I don't think I'll ever fly on Carpet
again.'

Tommy burst out laughing. 'Thank Gaw' it's only your
Aunt Pearl. When I hadn't seen you about for the past
few weeks I thought you'd been nabbed by the school
inspector.'

'School inspector?' said Kit.

'Yeh, that's what I'm doing up West. Trying to keep
out his way. He's already got Alfie and the twins and I
ain't seen a hair of 'em since. Makes you think don' it?

School never minded us not going before because we were always getting up to all sorts with our magic—like when Alfie gave Miss Battlestone a bright blue moustache. Now they sets this inspector on us like a blood'ound.' He shuddered. 'I had a nightmare about him last night, I did, scared me half to death.'

Ordinarily this piece of news would have fired Kit's imagination, perhaps enough to have organized a school inspector hunt or other similar game, but not today. The rain suddenly grew heavy and he pushed Tommy back into the shelter of one of the taller buildings.

'Listen, Tommy,' he said. 'I think Henry's in trouble. Real trouble. And it's my fault cos I let him get bit by the werewolf in the first place, so I have to help him, see? But to do that I need to borrow your broomstick.'

'Get away,' said Tommy, smiling in disbelief. 'My dad'll kill me if anything happened to my broom—it used to belong to him, so it's the nearest we got to a family heirloom.'

'It's important. *Please*, Tommy.'

Tommy peered closely at him through his thick spectacles. 'You ain't kidding me on none are you? Like the time Fin put treacle on my broom handle.' And he added darkly, 'You can still see where them wasps stung me.'

'I'm dead serious,' said Kit. 'Gang honour.'

Tommy blinked at him. 'Well . . . all right . . . I suppose. But you got to promise to send it back to me soon as you've done with it, or my dad really will make mincemeat out of me.'

'Promise.' Kit grinned with relief. 'I'll fly you home first if you want.'

'*What*, and come face to face with that mean ol' school inspector. No thanks. Put me down in the street, I'll feel safer with others about.'

81

A minute later Kit found a relatively clear patch of pavement to land on. Tommy slid off the back of the handle.

'You make sure Henry is all right,' he said. 'And don't forget to send my broomstick home—'

Kit took off so fast he didn't have time to call back. He streaked across the sky, weaving under and over blimps and rocking aircabs as he flashed by. Cabbies shook their fists, blared klaxons and called him a wild hooligan. But Kit never once slowed down, flying dangerously close to the propellers of several cloud-clippers, and only swerving around them at the final moment.

At last he reached Buckingham Palace, landed on the island and made his way underground into the building. He did not stop until he stood outside the nursery door listening to hear if Henry was alone. Hearing no voices, he turned the handle and went in. The room was in darkness. Kit marched over and wrenched back the curtains.

The sudden movement and light awoke Henry, he opened his eyes. 'Kit?' he gasped. 'How did you—'

Kit studied his friend, his face was waxen and his eyes like two dark holes.

'Get up,' he ordered briskly. 'Mr Sparks is not taking care of you any more—I am.'

Henry sat up wincing from pain. Kit helped him remove his pyjama jacket, then carefully unwound the bandage. Underneath, Henry's arm was purple and puffed up with poison which appeared yellow beneath the skin; the werewolf's bite-mark clearly visible too.

'Hold still while I put a little of this on,' said Kit, pulling a bottle from his pocket.

'Oh, it's cold and it tickles,' said Henry with a shiver. 'What is it?'

Kit's answer filled him with a warm sense of reassurance.

'Magic,' he said simply.

It was still raining hard when the two boys reached the island, climbing out beneath the statue of Pan. Previous to this, Kit had made sure Henry was dressed warmly and had on the right clothes to keep him dry; and then, when finally dressed and ready, Kit had written a quick note to explain that Henry would be back when he was fully better, and for this Kit promised to take all responsibility. They climbed onto Tommy's broomstick, Kit at the front, Henry behind—Henry only able to grip with one hand.

'I'll manage,' he said. 'And my other arm doesn't hurt half so much already.'

Kit wondered if he was telling the complete truth. 'Up and steady,' he growled at the broomstick, and it rose and flew off a good deal more sedately than it had arrived.

As they flew through the rain towards Piccadilly, Kit felt Henry's weak grip around his waist and wondered if he had really done the best thing for his friend. The next problem they faced was where were they to go? They couldn't very well fly around London in the rain all night. Kit thought about throwing himself onto the mercy of his aunt or even his father, but he knew exactly what would happen if he did. They would send Henry back to the Palace—back to the care of that madman Sparks.

So gently Kit flew the broom on until they had passed the fine white mansions and their well tended squares that from the air made London resemble a perfect chess board; past the department stores that stood lit up like palaces, and past the towers and steeples of the capital's best known landmarks. With his eyes fixed to the blue and white striped smog lighthouse at Stepney, Kit flew them east.

Soon the houses grew huddled together along mean cobbled streets, each house right up against the road, with a brick yard at the back scarcely big enough to hang a tin bath on a rusty nail. There were hardly any parks, and the only places to play were the wastelands which were numerous and overgrown. Lights shone through the dirty broken windows of grim factories; and the workers on the late shift bowed their heads and plodded miserably through the rain to clock on.

Kit hovered low. He called out to a man in a cloth cap, asking for directions to Plague Pit Lane.

'Down there on the left,' replied the man, without either stopping or bothering to glance up. He motioned sharply with his thumb.

'Er, thank—' But the man was gone.

'Plague Pit Lane,' said Henry over Kit's shoulder. 'It sounds disgusting, what on earth do you want there?'

'Fin's old man runs a shop in Plague Pit Lane,' answered Kit. 'And we need to find Fin. As I see it, he's about the only one who can help us.'

They moved slowly over wet, glistening cobbles and found the lane just as the man had indicated. It was every bit as unpleasant as its name suggested it would be—dark and narrow and twisting; and wasn't even wide enough for a pavement or lamp-posts, being lit instead by irregularly placed gas lamps high up on metal brackets; yet even so some of these were broken or little more than a low flickering flame that endlessly stirred the shadows rather than holding them back.

The shop of Fin's father, Bull Finnegan, was squeezed between a rowdy pub and a pawn shop. Outwardly it appeared to be an ordinary shop itself, although nothing was painted above the front window. However, over the door on a creaking chain hung a sign—an opened hand— which is the symbol of a moonshiner, and as easily recognizable as the three brass balls of the pawn shop next door.

Now moonshiners are the lowest of the enchanters. All other wizards and witches look down their noses at them, while one of the worst possible insults amongst magic folk is to say someone had *the magic of a 'shiner*. Moonshiners deal mainly in repairing old or leaky spells, they trade in second-hand charms and pieces of slipshod magic. They sell curses with no questions asked and are well known for a particular revenge spell called a *nipper* which will lurk in a dark alley for days waiting for its victim to show. Burglars bought noise mufflers off them and sellers of rotten meat bought stink sweeteners. Moonshiners gave magic everywhere a bad name.

Kit landed and he and Henry went through the door. A bell jangled and Kit jumped for he was more than a little nervous. He had never before set foot inside a moonshiner's and to do so now made him extremely uncomfortable, in the same way he imagined Aunt Pearl would be in the unlikely event of her ever visiting a gin palace.

Inside, the shop was quite bare. Old sawdust lay scattered on the floor before a plain wooden counter, and two glow-balls provided light. They sparked badly and swam with oily colours, which to Kit was a sure sign of indifferent magic; and over the counter casting its shadow across it hung a stuffed crocodile. As soon as the bell sounded, a curtain was swept aside and a man stepped out from a back room. He was unshaven and wore a filthy leather apron. He looked like a bigger, grosser version of Fin and was obviously his father. In his youth Bull Finnegan had been a bare knuckle boxer, and his nose had been broken so many times it was flat and shapeless.

'Well?' he asked leaning across the counter. 'What can I do for you fine pair of lords?' He grinned showing many

85

black and broken teeth. 'Maybe a nice winning love potion for your sweet'earts.'

Kit felt his face glow bright red. 'We don't need to buy nothing, just to see Fin,' he said fiercely and quickly.

Bull sucked spit through his rotten teeth and pulled himself up with effort. 'Fin! Fin!' he hollered up some wooden stairs. 'Get yourself down here quick. A pair of poshies have come to take you to tea at the Ritz.'

A moment later Fin clattered down the stairs, pausing halfway to peer at Kit and Henry.

'It's all right, Dad, they're only mates of mine,' he said ushering them from the shop. Once outside he suddenly rounded on them. 'What you two come here for?' he demanded.

'We need your help, Fin,' said Kit surprised at the hostile reception. 'We need somewhere safe to hide—just for a few days until Henry gets his strength back. After that we'll be ready to face what's coming to us.'

'What you on about, eh?' said Fin angrily. 'You had no right showing up here without the asking. No right at all.' He turned and glanced back into the shop, at his father who was watching keenly and ever so slightly nodding his head.

Henry touched Kit's shoulder. 'Perhaps we ought to go.'

'No,' said Kit firmly and he faced Fin. 'So you won't help us, is that it?'

'I never said that—did I say I wouldn't?' Fin waved his hand vaguely and looked miserable. 'All right,' he mumbled, 'if that's what you want—if that's what you want I'll see what I can do.' And he stared down at his scuffed boots.

While Kit and Henry remained on the street corner, Fin slipped back inside his father's shop. When he reappeared a few minutes later he wasn't wearing a coat but had slung a piece of old sacking over his shoulders, and of course had put on his pork-pie hat.

'No broomstick?' observed Kit in surprise.

'No . . . the place I know . . . it ain't far.'

'Best if I get rid of Tommy's broom then,' said Kit. 'You know how he frets about it, and I promised to send it back as soon as I didn't need it.'

Fin shrugged with indifference.

Kit pointed at the broom. 'Home,' he ordered; and the battered old broom leaning against the wall twitched into life and shot up with a crackle of magic. Watching it go, Kit couldn't help wishing he hadn't acted quite so rashly, but there was no calling it back, the broom was gone in seconds.

Then Fin said, 'Follow me and keep up.' He set off quickly and from the start made sure he was always a few paces ahead, seeming to distance himself from the risk of any awkward questions; not that Kit had any, he was more concerned about Henry.

'Slow down, Fin, for pity's sake,' he called when Henry began to cough. Fin hovered a moment, but still they never walked together as friends would.

The route Fin led them soon grew more complex than the maze at Hampton Court. Afterwards, if Kit had been asked to retrace his steps, he doubted whether he would have managed a quarter of the way with any confidence. Every dark alley was likely to divide into four different ones; while name signs, where they existed, said things like Snot Lane, Pass on Quick, and Choker's End.

'Is it much further?' asked Kit splashing through yet another puddle of stinking water.

'Through here,' came the flat reply; and Fin squeezed himself through a hole in a wall.

Previously there had always been some small light or other to see by, a low burning gas lamp or candle in a cottage window (the area was far too poor for electricity), but this new street, the one they now entered through the hole in the wall, was without a single spark from end to end. Slum houses, workshops, a seamen's lodge and even a tin chapel stood boarded up ready for the demolition gangs to move in with their mechanical nudgers and brick pulverizers; indeed some roofs were already open to the rain. The entire street felt and smelt like the bones of something that had died of neglect long ago—gables leaned, weakling elders sprouted from walls and ledges, and water gurgled eerily in broken pipes.

Henry started to cough again and Kit noticed him touch his poisoned arm.

'Kit, I'm so, so tired,' he said. 'Tired and cold.'

'Don't worry,' said Kit. 'Soon we'll find you a nice warm place as snug as any nest. You see. And then you'll be able to sleep all you want and I'll sit next to you and make sure that no one disturbs you . . . just a little longer, Henry.'

He went to point a glow-ball, but Fin beat him to it—then made the glow-ball rise and fall twice.

Why's he doing that? thought Kit. It looks like he's signalling. And before the danger signs could be properly read, something in the darkness stirred and a strong hand gripped his shoulder.

Chapter Eight

I t had been a trap all along! At first disbelieving and shocked, Kit soon boiled up ready to fight his way out of it.

'Let go of me, you . . . you . . . big ugly baboon!' he bawled, half escaped from his coat, his collar lost somewhere above his ears and buttons popping. He managed to squirm around and catch sight of Bull Finnegan's nasty red podgy face, and his fist thudded upon the moonshiner's chest. Bull didn't so much as blink.

'Listen up, boy,' he said in a low rasping growl. 'We can do this my way, nice and easy like—else I've got a pocketful of best nippers that hangs on worse than a barrel-load of crabs. They'll give you reason to squeal.'

But his threat made no difference whatsoever. Part of the reason for Kit's fury was Henry, who had been seized by an altogether more peculiar figure—tall, thin, smiling, with long milky fingers that you just knew would be damp and limp; he was dressed entirely in black, from the black shiny shoes on his feet to a black top hat on his head, carefully tied about with a piece of black satin.

'Come along . . . come along, my stray little lamb,' he urged Henry in a soft creeping whisper favoured by some undertakers—but here sounding far more sinister. Certainly Henry thought so. He put up no struggle against this thoroughly ghoulish creature and simply stared at him in horror.

Kit was frightened too, frightened and angry, which left

no room for magic. He lashed out with feet and fists, watched by Fin who hovered nearby, unsure where his loyalties lay. Should he go to the help of his father or to the help of his friends? At last he could stand it no longer.

'It weren't my fault, Kit!' he wailed. 'I wanted nothing to do with this. Only he made me—my old man made me do it. Gang honour, I ain't to blame none!'

'You do what I tell you,' snarled Bull. 'And be sharp about it if you know what's good for you. Now go bring up the horses, boy.'

Fin glowered at his father only to meet a much fiercer glower in return. Fin's defiance crumbled. Meekly he turned and ran off into a side alley, reappearing moments later leading a pair of sleek, shiny horses both as dark as midnight; and behind them a black windowless vehicle. The horses snorted and shook their proud heads, on each was a plume of black ostrich feathers somewhat spoilt by the rain.

'Get 'em on board,' ordered Bull.

'Aboard a hearse!' uttered Henry deeply shocked at the idea.

'My dear—my dear,' said the man in the black hat smarmily. 'You are quite mistaken. That isn't a hearse at all. Ho-no. That is a conveyance for carrying whatsoever I choose: and since what I choose to carry in my conveyance is not a coffin but you, my dear, and very much alive, my dear, it *ipso facto ain't no hearse*.'

His last few words came out harsher than he'd intended.

'You can say what you like but it's a hearse all right,' cried Kit, seeing a chance to rattle the fellow. 'It's a hearse with your name painted out because you don't want no one to know that you're an undertaker.'

'I am *not* an undertaker,' insisted the man. 'I am a

schools' truant inspector. We dress . . . we dress very similar to undertakers, and let it be said we take our work no less seriously. Your mistake is quite common, my dear, and—ha-ha—many is the amusing misunderstanding this has led to.'

'What rubbish,' sneered Kit, pushing his head between the moonshiner's great big hairy hands as they tried to stop up his mouth. 'School finished ages ago. You can't take us back there—we're not doing nothing wrong!'

The man smiled craftily. 'Ah, my dear, what you say is perfectly true for today but tomorrow—*tomorrow* I must make sure of your good attendance. Ah, such are the heavy responsibilities on the shoulders of a diligent inspector like myself.'

Henry was growing more and more alarmed. 'I don't want to go into a hearse with an undertaker,' he said loudly.

'Carriage, dear, carriage!' shrieked the man.

'Enough!' Bull's strong voice silenced them all. 'Get 'em on board and we've done for the night. Fin! Don't just loaf about as useful as a broken wand—go open the doors, boy!'

When Fin ran forward and opened the two doors at the back, he revealed that there was a second set behind them, and the second set was made of iron bars. Fin pulled these doors wide as well and Henry crawled inside without a murmur of protest.

The man in the black hat beamed. 'Excellent, my dear. I shall make a note of that in my report—the report I always write for the chief inspector. "Boy number one exceedingly co-operative" I shall say, "unlike boy number two . . ."'

He glanced worriedly at Kit, now thrown over Bull's shoulder. 'Out of the way,' said Bull coldly, and he tossed Kit after his friend.

Before all the doors were slammed shut, Kit had time to notice two things: that the inside of the hearse was really a cage and that he and Henry were not alone. Other pale faces blinked at them, too frightened to say a word. Then the doors were slammed shut and locked, and without windows Kit could make out nothing at all.

'Henry—where are you?' he called anxiously.

'Here, right beside you,' answered Henry. 'Don't worry, he didn't hurt me.'

Kit sparked at the very thought.

'Well, sit back, and the rest of you sit back too, I'm going to use my magic to blast the doors off their hinges—then we make a run for it.'

He brimmed with his old self confidence and magic; however a glum voice nearby said, 'Won't work . . . not with magic. Bull has the doors magic-proofed.'

To Kit's great amazement he recognized the voice at once. 'Tommy, but how—'

'Made the biggest mistake of my life, didn't I,' admitted Tommy mournfully. 'Soon after you'd gone I saw a steam wagon from the Chinese laundry just up my street, so I hops on the back of it thinking it will save me a walk home. But when I jumped off it and was taking my usual short-cut across the wasteground near to my house, this dirty great net lands over me and the next thing I know I'm banged up in here.'

Other voices murmured agreement—their stories pretty much similar.

Tommy sniffed. 'Tell me, did you send me old broom back home, Kit, like you promised?'

When Kit said he had, Tommy started to cry. 'Mother will worry when my broom arrives back without me. She'll think summat terrible has happened.'

'Summat has,' said a new voice, that of a girl. 'The truant inspector has nabbed you.'

'Poh, he's not a real truant inspector,' said Kit, 'just someone pretending he is and trying to fool us.'

'So,' said the girl, 'if he ain't no truant inspector—who the flip is he? And more to the point, what's he want with us?'

In the darkness Kit felt many eyes upon him waiting for an answer.

'I don't know,' he said quietly. 'I simply don't know.'

Pulled by its two black horses the hearse raced along at a very unhearse-like rate, the unrelenting rain pelting down on it, drumming on its roof like impatient fingers. Inside, Kit called up a glow-ball and poked around his head at the company. Besides himself and Henry he counted eight other youngsters. Tommy was sucking his thumb unashamedly, his eyes red and his spectacles skew-whiff where he had tried to rub beneath the lenses. The girl, whose name Kit overheard as May, had placed a comforting arm around Tommy's shoulders: she had dark curly hair and large teeth with gaps between them.

Seeing all he needed to see for the time being, Kit turned his attention to Henry, helping him to remove his coat.

'What's up with him then?' asked May bluntly after watching a while.

Kit, rolling back Henry's shirt sleeve, said, 'Been bit by a werewolf, hasn't he.'

'Liar! There ain't no werewolves in England.'

'*There are*,' said Kit fiercely, 'if you happen to know where to find 'em.'

Naturally everyone grew extremely curious, crowding around Henry, wanting to see what a werewolf bite actually looked like, and asking many questions. One raggedly dressed urchin whose damp clothes gave off a particularly bad smell, said, 'Here, mate, can I touch it?'

''Course not,' snapped Kit. 'You want to put germs into the wound?'

'What's germs?' said the boy with a shrug.

Watched with deep interest by the others, Kit rubbed a little more lotion on to Henry's arm; Henry closed his eyes, smiling.

'Coo, smells funny if you ask me,' said May wrinkling up her nose. 'Does it feel pecooliar?'

'It tickles,' said Henry. 'But in a nice way—like lemonade bubbles going up your nose.'

'There, all done.' Kit stoppered the bottle and as he did the hearse swerved violently to the side, sending them tumbling into a squealing heap.

'Oi—watch where you're going!' they heard Bull roar at another driver.

Then the undertaker's niggling voice arose. 'Perhaps, my dear, not quite so speedy—after all it wouldn't do to drive my you-know-what into the ground. Remember it's a tool of the trade and I shall need it for business when you-know-who no longer requires our services.'

Bull grunted but didn't slow down.

A little while later they finally stopped and Kit snuffed out his glow-ball with a pinch of his fingers.

'Where d'you think—' began Henry. Kit shushed him quiet; the doors were being opened. They swung apart and Fin appeared before them, rain streaming down his face. He seemed on the verge of saying something when Bull pulled him out of the way and thrust his own ugly mug into the hearse.

'Just to warn you there'll be no monkey business,' he said. 'I happen to know there's a couple of wizard bright sparks here who may think themselves above the likes of a ordinary working wizard like me. Well they ain't. Cos if they try it on any I got something very special waiting up me sleeve that'll make 'em truly wish they hadn't.' He glared meaningfully at Kit who felt his eager simmering magic sink down inside him to a brooding flame.

'Stay together and no laggers,' ordered Bull.

Kit helped Henry down, and as the other youngsters came creeping out after them they looked around with cowered heads at where they had been brought. It was a silent, dead-end lane, which except for the narrow way in was totally enclosed by tall dreary backs of buildings; each building covered in an unsightly mish-mash of pipes, with washing-lines strung between balconies. Yet the hearse had pulled up before none of these and stood close to a structure which resembled a squat factory chimney. They stared at it. It was brick and circular and over the door was painted: London Subterranean Railway Company—fan no. VIII.

Henry whispered into Kit's ear, 'But isn't this a ventilation shaft for the underground railway?'

Kit nodded discreetly.

Bull meanwhile had hurriedly selected a key from a large bunch and, all the time glancing around to see if he was being observed, unlocked the door.

'In you trot, my brave scholars,' called the undertaker cheerily. He had taken over the driving seat ready to set off. 'And remember, always work hard at your lessons. Ye shall reap what ye sow in the end, my dears. Remember that, it's a valuable lesson in itself.'

Bull, unimpressed by fine words, shoved the last few stragglers through the doorway. He followed behind and locked the door on the inside. Over their heads a huge fan turned eerily in the breeze. This was the top fan, a second lay far below near the bottom of the shaft; and during the day motors ran both fans continuously, cleaning out smoke and stale air from the underground lines. At nights, however, with no trains running, the fans were switched off, only coming on every now and again to prevent the build-up of foul air.

The shaft itself was hollow, except for a metal staircase on one side. Enclosed in a safety cage, the staircase zigzagged down in a series of landings, and made a steep daily climb for the railway workers who were forced to use it.

Bull prodded the air and a spinning, misshapen glow-ball appeared, greenish and covered in unsightly lumps like boils. Kit must have given it a superior glance for Bull said defensively, 'Does the job, don' it?' And then turned to Fin.

'You walk behind, boy, and give your old man a holler if any of 'em steps out of line. Specially Lord La-di-da over there. It'll be my pleasure to teach *him* a lesson.'

With a leer at Kit, Bull started down the metal stairs, his glow-ball following like a water filled balloon.

Kit took a defiant step after him, Henry caught his wrist.

'Wait, Kit, you'd be stupid,' he whispered. 'Don't let your temper get the better of you this time—it's what he wants.'

Kit squinted up his eyes. 'No, Henry, you're quite right,' he said. 'Let Bull say whatever he wants to me; you see, I won't raise so much as a spark back at him.'

'Glad to hear it,' said Henry, clearly relieved.

Nobody spoke as they filed down behind Bull, some youngsters were too over-awed at finding themselves here, and some too afraid, imagining what might be coming next. Whenever a breeze caught in the ventilation shaft it produced a ghostly hum—almost as if trying to form a word—and the topmost fan clattered and dim shadows flickered on the metal handrails.

'Keep moving down—keep moving down,' said Bull. He didn't need to raise his voice much above a whisper for them all to hear; and by the shifty way he kept glancing around, Kit knew he was as uneasy about this place as the rest of them.

Just then a distinct click sounded at the bottom of the shaft, and a few seconds later a similar click was heard overhead.

Bull grew edgier. 'Move back close to the wall,' he told them as they came down onto a landing.

'Why, what's a matter?' demanded Mary, not moving until she knew.

Bull didn't answer, so Fin said, 'It's the fans—they've come on.'

Voices broke out in alarm despite the moonshiner's attempts to reassure them.

'Ain't nothing to get steamed up about, not if you holds on tight,' he said loudly, while making sure he had a good, safe place in the corner.

Within a frighteningly short space of time both fans were whirling at speed, and the hot dry air which at first trembled unpleasantly began to flow upward, gathering force. Fin clutched his pork-pie hat to his head; elsewhere in the huddled little group, hair and collars and scarves were ruffled and snatched.

The air-flow rapidly grew stronger; it ran as powerfully as a mountain river, sucking words and shouts from opened mouths and adding them to its own deafening roar. From out of the dark depths newspapers, dust clouds, and old tickets went spiralling past; then, like magic gone wrong, Tommy, who was the smallest one there, was lifted clean off his feet, and before anyone was able to pull him back, he flew across as light as a leaf and became stuck halfway up the enclosing safety cage, his legs and arms pinned to his sides, his pockets emptying of conkers,

97

marbles and pieces of string, and his expression terror-struck.

Bull must have been getting afraid too, because suddenly he lost grip on his magic and his glow-ball vanished. Left in the howling darkness Kit and Henry clung on, Henry making do as best he could with his one good arm, but it was hard; and Kit next to him knowing he was unable to help him. For five long minutes this went on until the motors finally cut out and the suck of air grew noticeably less powerful. Tommy slid down from the cage, and the circling newspapers fluttered back to their underground roost.

Beyond a few lost buttons and grit in their eyes, none of them were any the worse afterwards, not even Tommy who searched desperately for bruises to show them. Bull sheepishly relit his glow-ball and they went on, past the second fan (now utterly still), through a door and onto a platform. Without pausing, Bull leapt down onto the tracks.

'It's all right,' he said when he saw their disbelieving faces. 'Ain't no trains at this time, is there.'

He made them line up along the platform's edge and one by one pulled them down beside him; but Kit made sure he jumped down first and helped Henry himself, this way he spared him from Bull's rough handling.

'Do you think you'll be able to keep up?' he whispered.

Henry smiled vaguely. 'I shouldn't have too much trouble if we go at a steady pace,' he said.

Tommy, busy studying his surroundings, had so far discovered nothing to like about them. 'Coo, it's like being stuck at the centre of the earth,' he said loudly, his voice echoing into the dark distance.

May folded her arms. 'Well, I ain't at all struck at having to stand here on these flaming railway lines.'

'Keep your mouth shut and walk,' said Bull, shoving her.

'Charming I'm sure,' said May huffily.

As a group they set off along a seemingly never-ending railway tunnel, following the moonshiner's lumpy, green light. Trouble was it managed to cast more shadow than anything, and they found it near impossible to see where they were going, especially those furthest from it. Before long a boy had tripped over a railway sleeper, and he landed so heavily that he grazed his shins and face. Bull stared at him unsympathetically; and when he told the boy he'd better be less clumsy next time, Kit was so irritated he wondered whether to risk a nipper or two by telling Bull exactly what he thought of him.

But then quite unexpectedly and dramatically the entire tunnel opened out into a gigantic cavern.

'It's a Burrower village,' gasped Henry, who being royal had never done anything so ordinary as travel on the Underground before and so had never seen its really quite common sights—except in books, which is never the same.

But he was right, it *was* a Burrower village, the railway crossing by it on a viaduct. It stood on a kind of rocky island with waterfalls brimming over many ledges at various heights behind it. Typically the tiny houses were richly decorated with curly fossils, while dinosaur bones did for beams in place of timber; and the houses were packed so closely together that their shale roofs formed a pleasing jumble, gable running into gable. At the edge of the village where narrow alleys met the foaming water, stepping stones or slab stone bridges led to deep circular ponds where fish were farmed, or else went further on to the foot-tunnels which opened as tall slits in the craggy rock face.

The Burrowers, a small, friendly people, have lived underground for such a length of time that they are no longer used to strong sunlight, but get all the light they need from a glowing quartz which occurs naturally (for instance as stalactites), or in some cases they dig up lumps and stand it on stone columns rather like lamp-posts. The quartz gives out a soft ice-coloured light, and coming into the cavern everyone's face immediately became tinged with blue.

The Burrowers had been discovered when the first underground railway was dug, yet they had been tunnelling beneath London for centuries before that; and when it was seen just how skilful a job they made of it, they soon became the Underground's chief builders, joining up their scattered villages before anyone could stop them; and while it was usual for above-ground people to pay tuppence for their train ticket, travelling Burrowers were permitted to pay in fish.

From the viaduct, Kit and Henry searched the village hoping to see some sign of a welcome.

'I don't think anyone is there,' said Henry disappointedly, for more than ever he felt a need to stop and rest.

Kit thought the village deserted too, but for Henry's sake he kept on searching.

Then they heard something which made them both turn away from the Burrower village and stare along the railway track. It was the toot of a distant train. Accusingly they rounded on Bull.

'You told us there weren't no trains!' exploded Kit.

'And here we are on this bridge stuck right and proper,' wailed Tommy. 'It's too high to jump off and anyway I can't swim if I did.'

The moonshiner came wading through the youngsters as if they didn't exist. 'That ain't right,' Kit heard him mutter. 'The whole line's supposed to be closed.'

100

He pointed at his glow-ball and it grew bigger becoming paler as it grew, eventually popping like an over-blown soap-bubble. He looked suddenly confused and turned around as if searching for a way to save himself . . . but even running was useless.

The train tooted again, sounding much closer this time than before; and they could hear the steady puff of steam. Then, before they knew it, the train had rounded a bend and two piercing lights shone straight into their eyes as it came hurtling towards them.

'Kit—use your magic,' said Henry, 'or the driver will never notice us in time.'

'Yeh, go on,' urged May bossily. 'For so many wizards about the place there seems precious little in the way of magic.' She stared hard at the moonshiner.

Without a word Kit strode up beside Bull Finnegan. He wasn't afraid but inside he was angry at Bull for having brought them into this danger in the first place. He wove all of that anger into his magic, calling up the biggest glow-ball he had ever created in his life, a monster of a thing that throbbed red with fury.

As soon as it appeared brakes squealed and sparks flew and a small pea-green engine slid, wheel-locked, onto the viaduct, getting closer and closer in an angry cloud of hissing steam.

'Oh, it ain't going to stop,' cried Tommy. 'We're going to be squashed!'

But it did stop . . . with only a few feet to spare. It stopped with a long dying hiss; and when he turned around, Kit was astonished to find Henry, May, Tommy, and all the others crouched behind him for protection.

'Didn't impress no one with that, boy,' sneered Bull regaining his old arrogance. 'It had already seen my light shining out a warning.'

Kit didn't pay him the slightest attention, he was staring open mouthed at the train, or rather at its driver who had just leapt down.

Kit saw it was no less a person than Stafford Sparks.

Chapter Nine

'Finnegan—where the devil have you been, man? I've ridden up and down this line for the past hour in this clapped-out tin-pot of a kettle on wheels looking for you.'

Bull lowered his head, clearly in awe of Sparks. 'Sorry, gov'nor,' he said. 'Got delayed.'

'Delayed—been lax more like. If this is what happens every time I'm not around no wonder we're so far behind.' He spoke to Bull like a schoolmaster does to a naughty schoolboy, Kit fully recognizing his tone. 'Well, Finnegan, for your information I shall be around a lot more from now on. You see, I no longer have to be a nursemaid to that spoilt brat up at the Palace.'

'Oh,' said Bull looking up. 'Is he well again?'

Sparks's eyes gleamed with pleasure. 'Even better—he ran away with that mad witch doctor's son, and good riddance to them both. Now less of the chat, man, let's see some movement. How many have you brought me tonight?'

'About ten, gov.,' said Bull apologetically. 'Would have been more but there ain't many of the little perishers about—on account of the rain keeping 'em at home by their fires.'

'Sure it wasn't keeping *you* at home by *your* fire, Finnegan?' said Sparks suspiciously.

Bull reacted suitably shocked and offended at the suggestion, so Sparks scowled and said, 'Get them in the back, we'll take them straight there.' He shook his head and added, 'Am I the only one who understands that time is running out on us? We need all the extra hands we can get.'

Eager to show himself loyal and willing, the moonshiner quickly bullied the youngsters along to an open wagon hitched to the rear of the train. Sparks, who was dressed as if he'd come from a night at the opera, a white silk scarf loose about his neck, stood wiping a spot of oil off his sleeve, not even bothering to glance their way—which was fortunate. He was bound to recognize Kit and Henry if he had.

Bull thumped the side gate bolt back into place.

'You not coming aboard, Dad?' asked Fin with a nervous swallow.

'I got important business to discuss with Mr Sparks up front,' replied Bull absently. Sparks obviously didn't agree, for he had already started the train, forcing Bull to run and throw himself onto the footplate.

Fin sat awkwardly in a far corner hugging his knees, the others shunning him as though he had something catching. Creating a big gesture of it, Kit turned his back on him, making sure Fin couldn't see what he was doing, which was running his fingers along the bottom of the wagon and blackening them with coal dust. Without a word of explanation he suddenly smeared his dirty fingers across Henry's cheek.

Henry pulled away. 'Hey! What are you playing at?'

'Keep still, Henry, you idiot, do you want Sparks to recognize you the next time he gives us a proper look? Now slip off your boots—that's it—they're far too smart. Here I'll scuff 'em about a bit for you—make 'em look good 'n' lived in.' He grinned.

Soon Henry joined in the spirit of the thing by dirtying Kit's face, and when it could be no blacker he attempted to flatten his distinctive mass of unruly hair. After all, Sparks was not likely to forget either in a hurry—not after their last meeting!

The beggar-boy who had asked to touch Henry's wounded arm eyed Henry's fine, tweed coat enviously. 'If that's your line of thinking,' he said, 'I'll obligingly swap my coat with his, and be glad to have been of service.'

'No thank you,' said Henry, coolly regarding the dirty rags on offer to him.

'But you must do something with that coat,' agreed Kit. 'It makes you stand out a mile. Here—'

Seizing one of Henry's pockets he gave a sharp tug and ripped it half off.

'Cor, can I have a go?' begged Tommy; and before Kit could reply the other pocket hung down like a dog's ear too; and with a bit more dirt and a few more well placed tears here and there, Henry's transformation into a ragamuffin was complete.

'That should do the trick,' said Kit admiring his handiwork; then he glanced over his shoulder, adding, 'Unless someone happens to give us away.'

Fin shifted uncomfortably. 'All right, Kit, I can't say I blames you any for hating me. But I'm only doing what I'm made to do—don't have to like it any more than the rest of you.' And he muttered, 'Bull mightn't be much of one, but he's still my father.'

Kit stared at him calmly, not hating him at all. This flustered Fin even more.

'Look, for what it's worth I can tell you this, you'll not be hurt. None of you will. Just keep quiet and do as you're told and in a bit you'll be set free. Ask yourselves—what's a few days of your life anyway? Besides, then you'll be in all the newspapers—famous no doubt—and you'll never have to see my ugly old mug ever again. See, Dad's taking me away soon as Mr Sparks pays him. Going on a Zeppelin 'cross to America we are, a cabin apiece says my dad. He's got these big ideas, see, gonna sell cheap fire-water magic to them Indians out there—' He broke off with an unnatural laugh.

Kit spoke quietly. 'Fin, what is Mr Sparks up to?'

Fin looked as if he was struggling to keep his answer back, like nothing good would come of it if he let it out.

'He's pretending to do grand things on the Underground, only he ain't,' he said darkly. 'Instead he's digging a tunnel—a tunnel to the Bank of England. He's going to steal all the bank's gold and most probably ruin the whole country into the bargain.'

'But nobody can get into the Bank of England, it's like a castle—it's like the Tower of London—' began Kit, who stopped, remembering that *they* had got into the Tower.

Henry was angry. 'After all the kindness Grandmama has shown him—'

'Oh, it gets worse,' Fin quickly went on. 'Once he has the gold, ol' Sparks can lay his hands on the best and fastest airships there are. A fleet of 'em bristling with cannon. And any country that won't pay him what he wants he'll bomb their ships and bring down their airships till they do. Soon nothing will be able to move without his permission—nothing in the whole world.'

Their journey in the little train was a brief one. At the very next station it pulled up at a long curving platform; and seeing the gas lamps burning and hearing the bustle of people, Kit was fooled into thinking that here at least the Underground was working normally. But nobody waited on the platform to catch a train; and on the opposite side he noticed a large hole in the tiled wall: it was from here that all the noise was coming. Without doubt this was the tunnel Fin had told them about, the one Sparks was digging to the Bank of England; and it couldn't be so very

106

far away either because the station was named 'Bank' after it.

The air was dusty and immediately set Henry coughing. May told him and the others to tie handkerchiefs over their mouths and noses if they found it too bothersome.

'Ain't got no hanky,' piped up the ragged urchin. 'Got a sleeve instead.' And he happily showed them how he used it.

'Down, the lot of you,' snarled Bull, unhitching the side gate. 'Er, shall I put 'em straight to work, Mr Sparks?' he asked when the train had emptied and the youngsters stood huddled together in a small group on the platform.

'Well, I haven't brought them all the way down here for a pleasant picnic,' replied Sparks sarcastically. He bit the end off a cigar and spat it on the ground.

Bull began pushing the youngsters along the platform. When level with the hole, Kit was surprised to see the tunnel behind it stretched about a hundred yards from the station. At its face a great number of figures worked heroically with spades and picks—Burrowers most probably: it was difficult to be absolutely certain because those that did the heavy or unpleasant work were grey from head to foot with clay. Other little grey figures shovelled up the spoil into carts that yet other little grey figures pushed along rails to the mouth of the tunnel and up a ramp, before finally emptying them onto a line of waiting railway wagons. These could be shunted away when full.

The tunnel was lit by powerful wheeled gas lamps (but not strong enough to hurt the Burrowers' sensitive eyes); while the tunnel's roof and sides were propped up with all manner of timber oddments. Overseeing the work were some twenty grim-faced men, standing as tall as giants amongst the Burrowers and youngsters; and slung over each one's shoulder was a rifle.

By the time Kit had seen all this and more, his group was down on the tracks, squeezing its way between the spoil wagons and about to enter the bustling tunnel.

Henry was still helpless with coughing.

'Make certain you stay close to me,' hissed Kit, grabbing tightly at his coat.

Jobs were being given out, usually in pairs. Tommy and May had been given a cart to push; Henry and Kit were told to take the next one.

Henry moved slowly into position. 'Honest, Kit, I shall try my best,' he said, 'but with this arm I feel next to useless.'

'Don't worry,' Kit reassured him. 'I can easily manage by myself; besides you'll only get in the way. You go sit and wait for me on that wall over there and I'll come by to get you the first moment I'm free.'

'Don't talk silly, Kit.'

'I'm not,' said Kit fiercely. 'Listen, I promised your grandma in that letter we left behind at the Palace that I would take best care of you, and so I shall if you listen to what I say.'

'Well, if you're sure—I mean *really* sure . . . '

'Gang honour,' said Kit and he spat on the ground.

Feeling somewhat guilty, Henry moved off and sat where Kit had told him. A few moments later Sparks was upon the scene, rushing up like a savage terrier.

'What's the matter with you, boy?—you haven't even started yet. Up up, on your feet I say. You've been given a job now make sure you do it.'

'Leave him be, mister,' called Kit disguising his voice. 'My brother's sick—got a dicky heart. If you make him do anything like this it'll do him in, and that'll add murder to your list of crimes, as well as kidnapping.'

Sparks was unmoved. 'There's no room for idlers. I need every cart working and it takes two brats at each one.'

As Henry was about to get to his feet again, a voice called, 'Here, I'll take his place, Mr Sparks.'

Kit turned around. 'Fin,' he said in surprise.

'Who are you?' asked Sparks suspiciously.

'Fin Finnegan,' he answered cheerfully. 'Bull's lad—and see I'm big 'n' beefy and as strong as a carthorse, Mr Sparks, worth two of him any day.' He nodded across at Henry.

Sparks shrugged. 'Very well, but don't expect special treatment because you're Finnegan's boy,' he said turning and walking away.

A guard stepped up and banged the cart with his rifle butt. 'Get it rolling,' he ordered.

They trundled the empty cart down the tunnel, passing a couple of guards who were too busy smoking and talking in low voices to notice them, yet out of habit would now and again break off their conversation to snarl, 'Come on—get a move on,' at no one in particular. Coming the opposite way on a parallel set of tracks were the full carts. Kit saw May and Tommy returning, but Tommy kept his head down, not daring to glance his way in case it landed him in trouble.

At the end of the tunnel a group of filthy workers stood ready to fill each empty cart as it arrived. One paused, his shovel half raised.

'Kit! Fin!' he said astonished.

'Who's that?' said Fin jumping as if a ghost had touched his shoulder.

Using the inside of his collar the figure wiped a clean patch on his dirty face.

'Alfie? That you?' asked Kit, still unsure.

Alfie nodded but didn't laugh as he normally would. His eyes were dull and his mouth was drawn tight. 'It's me all right,' he said. 'Gus and Pixie are here too. But it's not good, Kit. We ain't nothing but slaves.'

'For the moment maybe,' said Kit. 'Later we'll get together—all of us—and with our magic combined we'll burst our way out of this dump—we'll do it quicker than gunpowder.'

Kit's bright determination met Alfie's blank stare.

'Later you won't have enough energy to light a match,' he said. 'You'll be dead on your feet.'

Seeing them talking and not working, a guard began to make his way over. Alfie in a fit of fright began shovelling up clay for all he was worth, and the guard shrugged his rifle back up onto his shoulder and drifted away.

Deep underground the tunnelling went on all through the night, only stopping shortly before the clerks, office juniors, secretaries, and bankers arrived for another day's work. Despite falling behind with the digging, Sparks could not afford to risk their being heard now they were this close to the vaults.

Practically dropping with weariness, Kit still hurried to find Henry, who was asleep on the ledge where he had left him. Kit shook him awake.

'Can we go home now?' asked Henry, not yet fully out of his dreams.

'Soon,' promised Kit.

The guards herded the exhausted prisoners to a long cage on the platform, which being part of Bank station had old pennies and farthings set into it for decoration. Fin followed close behind, going through the barred opening with Kit, Henry, and the rest of the gang, being as unrecognizably dirty as they were; and when he heard Bull angrily calling his name to go home with him, he steadfastly refused to answer.

Slowly he took off his hat and wiped his brow along

his sleeve. 'Never wanted to go to America in the first place,' he mumbled.

Then the cage door clanged shut and was locked.

'Kit—Kit.' It was Alfie again. 'See, what did I tell you—Pixie and Gus—the twins. Only now we're more like triplets—I bet not even our own mothers could tell us apart.'

Alfie presented two clay-covered figures who could have been anyone if it wasn't for their identical smiles.

'So the gang is back together again,' said Kit.

'And don't forget me,' said May, pushing her way through and sitting down amongst them. 'I'm May, by the way—how d'you do. You can tell me your names back if you're feeling sociable, but I can't claim I'll recognize your faces.'

A guard called Bates brought food, which was surprisingly good—cold sausage and potatoes and chunks of cheese. There was fish for the Burrowers; and clean water for everyone to drink.

'He ain't so bad,' whispered Gus as Bates paced by the cage. 'Leastways he don't treat you like something scraped off the bottom of his boot.'

Bates had stopped to watch a Burrower amuse himself with a lump of clay, skilfully moulding it into a fish-shaped pot, its tail a handle, its mouth a spout. Clearly Bates was impressed by it and the Burrower held it up for him to view better. Bates stroked his chin and nodded; he crossed to a chocolate vending machine, kicked it viciously and collected what dropped out at the bottom. When he returned he offered the Burrower a penny chocolate bar in exchange for the fish, the Burrower indicated three bars and eventually they settled on two. But when the clay fish was passed to him, it seemed to fall apart in his hands. With a curse, Bates threw it down and stamped on it; the Burrower, who by this time had

111

shared the chocolate amongst all his children, watched, grinning and nodding.

'And *he's* one of the better ones?' marvelled Kit. 'What I don't understand is why Bates and Sparks and the rest of their crew have got us kids down here in the first place?'

'Kids are easy to bully and push around, ain't they?' said Pixie chewing on a sausage.

'And poor East End kids are rarely missed,' added Alfie. 'They run away and go missing all the time. And even if our mothers and fathers worry about it, it'll be a long while afore they gets over their natural mistrust and goes reporting it to the police, by which time Sparks will have done with us.'

Kit nodded towards the cage door. 'Magic-proofed, I suppose?'

'Fin's old man seen to that,' said Alfie. 'He's magic-proofed just about everything.'

Fin winced.

'Not that we blame you or nothing, Fin,' added Alfie hurriedly. 'I'm just saying—and for a 'shiner he's done a pretty good job of it too, we've all had a try at picking the lock, but somehow Bull's got his hands on some really strong magic and ours don't do nothing against it.'

Kit looked doubtful.

'He's right, Kit, it's true,' said Pixie. 'We even had a go at making our own wands out of scraps of wood.' And she couldn't resist adding, 'Gus's wand caught fire.'

Her brother stuck out his tongue at her.

'See, Mr Sparks told Dad not to scrimp on his magic like he norm'ly does,' explained Fin. 'He knew sooner or later witch and wizard kids were bound to turn up, and he didn't want 'em causing no trouble.'

Gus scowled. 'I tell you that Stafford Sparks is a bit harsh on magic all round. When he finds out I was a wizard he made sure I had one of the hardest jobs of all.'

'Huh!' Pixie was about to argue that her job was no less hard than her brother's when Bates pushed his face up to the bars. 'You sprogs best get your heads down now,' he said. 'One more day to go—but believe you me, it's going to be a murderous long slog.'

As with the food, blankets were plentiful for everyone, not that it was really cold on the Underground. The blankets were horrible and itchy, however, and May complained that hers smelt of horses. Before finding a place to lie, Kit rubbed a little more lotion on to Henry's arm.

'Thanks, Kit,' said Henry quietly, 'I really do feel a lot better for the way you've taken care of me and not just my arm—all of me. It sounds odd but somehow I know I shall never have to go on another rest-cure again.'

Kit gave it a moment's thought. 'Prob'ly that's some good coming from the werewolf's bite,' he said. 'Sometimes it takes a poison to fight a poison, at least that's what Aunt Pearl used to say, though it's a risky way to cure anyone.'

He sounded very serious, and Henry looked at him and smiled. 'You know, Kit,' he said, 'one day you're going to be every bit as brilliant a witch doctor as your father.'

The mention of his father brought Kit up with a jolt. He had pushed him to the back of his mind for so long.

'Why do you say that?' he asked curiously.

'Because it's true,' replied Henry. 'You're both so alike . . . G'night to you, Dr Kit Stixby, may you dream pleasant dreams of your green top hat.'

'Shut up, you idiot, and go to sleep,' said Kit smiling.

The gang lay close together and were nearly asleep when Tommy let out a deep, sad sigh.

'I wonder what my ma is thinking about now,' he said. 'She'd go to the police—storm right into the station and bang on the sergeant's desk she would, then call out the fire brigade for good measure. Why, she'd have the whole blooming navy sailing up and down the Thames if she thought they'd be useful . . . my old ma . . . '

May put her arm around him. 'You have a little sleep, dear,' she said. 'You take my word for it, things'll look much brighter after a nap.'

Tommy closed his eyes and instantly dropped off; and within five minutes not one of the gang was left awake.

Stafford Sparks paced back and forth along the platform, smoking a cigar, pausing only to pick tobacco from his teeth; behind him many sleeping forms lay huddled beneath blankets. There was something restless in the way Sparks moved and he nervously toyed with the little silver spanner on his cravat. Hearing someone approach he stopped and suddenly looked relieved.

'Ah, Bates. Did all go to plan?'

Bates nodded. 'We tricked the old woman down like you said, Mr Sparks. We sent word that someone was ill and in need of her magic.'

Sparks pulled an expression of extreme distaste. 'She came, of course?'

'Yeh, and we were ready for her. We made sure her hands were quickly tied behind her back so she couldn't point and use her . . . powers. She never stood a chance.'

'Excellent. Where is she now?'

'We left her at the station tied to a chair in the stationmaster's office. It's a shame we couldn't tie her tongue too, it gave us a rare old lashing.'

'That's these magic types for you—all hot air and little else.'

Bates chuckled then stopped. 'Boss, what about her pet monsters?' he asked uneasily.

'The gargoyles?' Sparks smiled. 'Don't worry, Bates, I've told you, without her presence there's not a single thing they can do to us. Oh, they may hiss and growl, but they need the witch to control them.' He puffed happily on his cigar. 'The way is clear, Bates, we can come and go to the tower whenever and as often as we like. Now see about food and water for our little guest workers here, in another hour it will be time to wake them up and send them back to work.'

The two men walked off and when they had gone, a face stirred from beneath the blankets. It was Kit trying to make sense of what he had just overheard. There couldn't be any possible mistake, it was Aunt Pearl they had been discussing—who else could it be? The tower and the gargoyles were proof. But what was she to them in all this? And why did Sparks require her tower so urgently?

Chapter Ten

K nowing he had precious little time, Kit shook his head free of last sleepy cobwebs. He needed to think clearly. He turned to the wall at the back of the cage where there was a map of the complete Underground system, Central Line in red; quickly he located Bank station upon it, the stop before he noticed being Yom, the Burrower village they had passed through; after Bank the next stop marked was St Paul's station where Sparks must be keeping Aunt Pearl his prisoner.

Sure of this, Kit sent his mind walking—

Or rather it ran in haste, slipping through the bars of the cage and down the main railway tunnel.

I don't want to go, I'm afraid of the dark, it complained. *Go on, don't be a baby, there's nothing in this tunnel that can harm you*, it answered at exactly the same time.

Kit, an empty shell without his mind, lay perfectly still under his blanket as if sleeping. This was taking all of his wizardly powers and he knew how dangerous it was to send his mind walking so far. If he lost control—even for a moment—his mind might drift away never to return, a case of really losing his mind; and the further it travelled from him the weaker became his control over it.

Then to his great relief it reached the next station.

No living thing was upon the platform, so it began to search the various rooms leading off it.

Is anyone here?

Unlike animals with their simple straightforward

116

brains, a wizard cannot pass into another person's head without first gaining permission; it is also considered polite.

Aunt Pearl—are you there?

Suddenly Kit's mind was thrown into a panic. It fluttered up like a startled pigeon, then raced out of the building, off the platform, and along the tracks into the tunnel.

Something close behind gave chase. As he lay still, Kit's eyelids twitched and his breathing grew rapid.

With a jump his mind leapt back into him. A moment later something was knocking on his skull, demanding to be admitted.

You let me in, my no-good nephew. You hear? It's no use hiding from me.

Kit's eyes flickered open and he smiled.

Aunt Pearl, he said; and he let her in at once.

To begin with Aunt Pearl was so angry that she stomped back and forth in his head, while Kit's own mind curled up into his memory waiting for her to calm down.

If ever I find out you're anything to do with these despicable people . . . I'll . . . I'll . . . disown you. I'll snub you in the street. I'll send you curses through the post on your birthday.

Aunt, said Kit. *Whatever you may think of me, I'm not one of Stafford Sparks's gang or anything to do with his plans.*

Stafford Sparks? said Aunt Pearl crossly. *You mean that nasty little man at the Palace who hates magic? What's he to do with any of this? . . . Oh, I suppose you'd better tell me everything from the beginning and hurry up about it, I'm an old woman and it's not good for me to be out of my body for so long.*

Kit told her his story and all he knew, starting with how he had tricked poor old Mr Pickerdoon.

I hope you realize, said his aunt sternly, *that your sleeping spell was so strong that he slept non-stop for seventeen hours!*

117

Kept quoting Shakespeare at me in his sleep, he did. Most disconcerting.

Despite everything, Kit couldn't stop himself smiling as he imagined it.

Cease smirking, child, and get on with it.

Kit continued, telling her how he'd rescued Henry, sought help from Fin, was captured and taken underground; and how Stafford Sparks was going to steal all the gold from the Bank of England and how he meant to use it.

The man's completely off his head, declared Aunt Pearl.

Maybe, replied Kit. *But for some reason your tower is important to him. That's why he wanted you out of the way— without you there'll be no one to let loose the gargoyles at his gang.*

I was manhandled by them, complained Aunt Pearl. *Oh, how I'd love to see those bullies jump to an old witch's magic— this old witch's magic in fact, but my hands are tied behind me. And let me tell you such are the people we're dealing with that the rogues pulled the rope as tightly as they could, and me a defenceless old woman. What's the matter with these creatures, don't they have mothers?* She stopped suddenly. *What about you, child, are your hands free?*

Yes, admitted Kit. *But everything here has been spell-proofed; and you are too far away for me to perform physical magic. I can't help you, Aunt, I'm afraid.*

Pity, mused his aunt.

Suddenly Kit had an idea, and the violence of his brainwave nearly knocked his aunt clean from his head.

Really—youngsters today, she huffed indignantly.

Come on, Aunt, said Kit, *I'll walk my mind back up the tunnel with you—then I'm off to find an old friend.*

Kit's mind pushed through the darkness, growing tired. It had been away from his body too long and was at the absolute limit of his control. Kit knew it was risky going on much longer, yet just as he was about to pull it back, his mind strayed into the head of the very thing it was searching for—

Hungry-hungry-hungry. Eat-eat-eat . . .

Hello.

Ekk! Don't do that! You give Rat his big fright. See—see, all fur stick up like when he see a monster pussy-cat.

Kit apologized. *Listen,* he said, *I need your help again.*

What you give Rat this time? asked Rat craftily.

As much food as you can eat and that's a promise.

Rat, he like those—what-you-call-its?—Bis-cuits.

Then I'll make sure you get hundreds of 'em. Now quickly, Rat, let me show you where you need to go.

Aunt Pearl was being unexpectedly difficult.

He's only a rat, Aunt, he won't harm you, spoke Kit's mind in a tone of strained patience.

Only a rat! Look at it sitting in front of me with those mean little hard eyes and those nasty scratchy claws and that pink nose and those long whiskers forever twitching. It quite gives me the vapours, I can hardly catch my breath. Never could I abide rats, even as a girl when cousin Bartrum used to change my pet toad into one. A big black brute it was. I used to scream until I was hoarse.

Really, Aunt, how can you say this when your gargoyles—

Don't you dare say another word, said his aunt crossly. *I won't have you compare those dear, sweet, gentle creatures to that . . . that . . . thing over there. If this is the sort of company you keep these days, nephew, it's little wonder you're always in such trouble!*

The rat, sensing he was being spoken about and believing it could only be in complimentary terms, opened his mouth in what another rat would understand to be a cheesy grin.

119

'Aggghh!' screamed Aunt Pearl, noticing only a gaping jaw and pointed teeth.

The rat bolted into a corner, suddenly as much afraid of Aunt Pearl as she was of him.

Kit nearly lost his temper.

Now just you listen here, Aunt Pearl, he said sternly. *Rat is your only way of escape, and unless you want to stay tied up forever you'll go across and apologize to him this very minute.*

Apologize? To a rat? You don't apologize to rats you put down poison for them. She shuddered. *No, what you say is quite, quite impossible, nephew.*

Kit sighed. *Then I suppose I must do it. Now close your eyes and don't look if you're so frightened—I'm off to promise more biscuits as a peace offering.*

Aunt Pearl closed her eyes as Kit had told her, but this made matters worse, so she opened them again only to find that Rat had vanished. Desperately she searched the floor in the firm belief that seeing Rat was preferable to not seeing him at all, for now she imagined him everywhere.

Suddenly she stiffened with terror, and it took all of her effort to stop herself letting loose another piercing scream. Behind her something large and hairy with oh-so tiny scrabbly feet was sniffing around her wrists.

A moment later Rat began biting at the thick cord that bound them. He made short work of it too; while all the time Aunt Pearl managed to sit perfectly still. But then this was hardly surprising—she had *fainted*.

Kit waited patiently beside Aunt Pearl's mind, which lay cold and shivering on the floor of her brain. Sluggishly it roused itself.

Has the rodent gone? she groaned.

Kit assured her that Rat had done his job and was no longer present.

Aunt Pearl gave a violent shiver then was back to her old self.

At last, she said, rubbing her wrists. *The moment I've waited for. Free to go and teach Mr Stafford Sparks and that rowdy crew of his a good long lesson in manners. Doesn't like magic, does he? Well, excuse me if I give him such a scorching—*

No! cried Kit. *You don't do nothing of the sort, Aunt. Mr Sparks's men have guns, you will be putting yourself in too much danger. Stay where you are, Aunt Pearl—please! There is a right time and a wrong time for magic, you always told me this. Trust me, I'll let you know when the time is right.*

Chapter Eleven

Kit brought his mind back just in time. Henry was hovering over him.

'I had a job to wake you,' he said. 'You must have been having a good dream.'

'Yes, in a funny sort of way,' smiled Kit. He sat up awkwardly, getting used to his body again, which felt like old leather boots that hadn't been worn in a long while—tight and restricting.

Bates had brought food—milk, dry bread, and lumps of cold ham—and May was bustling about making sure everyone received his fair share and watching over Tommy until he drank up all of his milk.

'Blimey, she's worse than my old ma,' he beamed delightedly.

In low muttered voices they ate their food while Bates paced in front of the cage, stuffing the last of the stolen chocolate bars into his mouth—drooling down his chin in his greedy haste to devour them.

Still, Pixie stared at him in envy. 'What I wouldn't give for a taste of that choc'late,' she sighed wistfully. She sat close to Gus, as close as two twins could be, and it appeared to Kit that they lifted their food and chewed as if one was the shadow of the other.

Nearby, Alfie and Fin exchanged whispers, the crouched, defeated Fin of yesterday no longer present, and Alfie managing to raise a chuckle and look rather more like the Alfie of old.

Gazing further along the cage, Kit noticed other

little groups of youngsters sitting and eating together like he and his friends, and also families of Burrowers. Somehow the Burrowers seemed a lot cleaner than the youngsters (perhaps knowing how to spruce themselves up is something that comes naturally after centuries of dealing with the grey sticky clay). With their thick ginger hair and green eyes, the Burrowers looked very striking: the men with long beards and many of the women carrying sleeping babies strapped to their backs; and unlike the youngsters the Burrowers ate fish, for they no longer cared for the taste of meat.

Seeing him stare, one particular Burrower winked his green eye at Kit and Kit smiled back, neither one understanding a single word of the other's language, but in this instance not really needing to. Then, feeling someone nudge him in the back, Kit turned around to see Henry grinning at him.

'See,' said Henry bending up his arms like a circus strongman to show how much better he was. Probably just as well: it was unlikely he would escape work a second time, this being the big push to complete the tunnel.

When Henry rolled up his sleeve the werewolf bite appeared no worse than a large bruise, and Henry himself rubbed the last of Kit's lotion into it.

'A full recovery,' he declared when done.

'But don't you go overdoing it just yet,' warned Kit.

'Don't worry, I shan't,' said Henry. He lowered his voice. 'Look out, Kit—here comes Sparks.'

Sure enough Sparks had arrived on the scene and was glaring through the bars. 'Why aren't they at work?' he shouted at Bates. 'Do I have to remind you to do *everything*? They can laze around all they like once the job is done.'

Bates hurriedly unlocked the cage and those who hadn't finished their breakfasts (or was it suppers?) quickly stuffed what they could into their mouths.

Pixie groaned and pulled her brother to his feet, then they all shuffled out, across the tracks and into the tunnel opposite, where the newly lit gas lamps had not yet reached full brightness and it was cold and shadowy.

Kit and Henry moved to take up a position behind a cart, Fin having already agreed to go and work alongside Alfie at the loading end. From the very start Kit sensed a new tension in the tunnel, the guards watching every movement for an instant of slackness, and Sparks yelling and criticizing—nothing ever good or fast enough for him. And Kit wondered why it was so necessary to finish the tunnelling work tonight. Then he thought of Aunt Pearl.

'Kit . . . Kit . . . '

Kit became aware that Henry was talking to him.

'Umm?'

'Are you all right?' asked Henry glancing at him in concern. 'You seem very odd—sort of, I don't know, *dreamy* I suppose.'

Kit smiled mysteriously. 'Prob'ly because I haven't got used to being m'self yet.'

'*What?*'

'I'll tell you about it as we work,' whispered Kit. 'Come on, that guard's giving us terrible black looks, we better get our backs into it.'

Henry sighed. 'If only Grandmama could see me now,' he said. 'She wouldn't be at all amused.'

The digging and the loading, the conveying and the tipping out of clay got into a steady rhythm, driven by the dull thud of pickaxes, the scrape of shovels, and the squeak of rusty wheels.

After Kit had told Henry about Aunt Pearl they rarely spoke again, although naturally Henry was delighted.

Silently they worked on for several long, back-breaking hours until Kit realized something quite strange had occurred.

He straightened up, listening, and the cart dwindled to a standstill, forcing May and Tommy who followed with the next cart to stop too. Yet no one shouted at them to get a move on as they might have expected, and this they were surprised to learn was because there wasn't a single guard nearby.

'And the picks and shovels aren't working either,' said Kit scratching his head.

Sure enough it was true, and as the rest of the carts ground slowly to a halt an eerie silence filled the tunnel. The guards, it could now be seen, were all together at the far end—at the face of the tunnel, clustered around something. Suddenly they and everyone else there started to run back as fast as they could, crouching down at a distance behind carts or heaps of clay.

'We better get our heads down too,' Kit told those around him. He wasn't sure why exactly, except it seemed a wise precaution to take.

As they huddled behind their carts a powerful muffled boom shook the ground. Nuggets of dry clay rattled down from the roof and the supporting timbers creaked; even the heavy carts squeaked and swayed a little.

'Sparks must have blasted his way into the Bank—' began Henry, who immediately broke off as an evil swirling cloud of dust swept down the tunnel engulfing everything like a desert sandstorm, forcing him (along with everyone else) to cover his eyes, nose, and mouth.

It took nearly ten minutes before the worst of the dust had settled—including upon them in a thick white coat! Then, crusty eyed and blinking hard, Kit forced himself to peer down the tunnel again. He was just able to make out a hazy figure stumbling towards him.

125

'Sparks,' he gasped, coming to recognize the face half hidden behind a mask and set of goggles.

Sparks was clutching something to his chest as tenderly as a new-born baby. Kit stared hard at it.

It was gold, he saw at last. A single, dusty, solid bar of gold.

Before the gang's excitement could get the better of them, Stafford Sparks took a firm control of the situation.

'Men, don't get carried away and lose your heads!' he roared. 'The gold isn't yet ours. Listen to me! It won't load itself onto the train and we go against the clock, each minute as precious to us as anything stacked up in that vault. Time has come to work fast and think clear, or I don't give a brass ha'pence for our chances.'

Instantly the men forgot their stupid grins and whoops and frenzied back slapping and each one nodded calmly.

Sparks set the example to follow, becoming as active as a demon. He barked orders and ran back and forth, knocking down anyone who stood in his way. Kit and his friends along with all the other slave workers were pushed and threatened until they formed a line—a human chain—which stretched all the way from the top of the tunnel, which now broke through into the vaults of the Bank of England, to a waiting train at the station end: Kit and his gang placed somewhere in the middle.

Minutes later the first bar of gold came down the line to Kit, and when it did he nearly dropped it, not realizing how heavy pure gold really is. Another bar followed close behind, and another and another . . . Kit reached sixty then lost count.

'Come on—come on,' urged Sparks racing up and down the line. Nervous sweat glistened upon his top lip.

Gold bar after gold bar passed through Kit's hands. He would have liked to stop to examine one more closely, but Sparks was growing more and more impatient, glancing at his pocket watch; comparing the time to another watch and both times to yet a third watch.

And then the gold simply stopped flowing.

'Get them back in their cage,' growled Sparks.

The prisoners were marched smartly back to the platform, Bates locked the cage door and pocketed the key. For a joke he pulled sixpence from his jacket and tossed it through the bars. Nobody moved to pick it up, everyone just stood staring in deepest contempt at his idiotic smirking face.

Somewhat shaken, Bates hurried away.

By now the train and its lone wagon were crowded with Sparks's men. They filled the cab or sat perched upon the heaps of gold. Bates was last aboard, hauled on by his collar and sleeves; then the train pulled slowly away. Passing the cage it gave a final triumphant toot and the men cheered madly, punching their fists in the air.

'It's not fair!' cried Gus shaking the bars and almost crying. 'They can't just get away easy like that.'

Alfie lobbed a curse at the train, but groaned with disappointment as it sparked lamely and fell by the wayside, no better than a dud firework. As might have been expected the train was heavily magic-proofed, and casting curses at it was like throwing feathers on a fire.

Then sensing something wrong much closer by, Pixie turned around and gave a little gasp. 'Gaw', what's happened to Kit?'

Henry was bending over him, and Kit's eyes had rolled back until they showed only whites. Everyone grew concerned.

'Is he having a fit?' asked Fin.

Henry looked up at them and smiled. 'Nothing to worry about,' he said cheerfully. 'Kit won't be long. He's only popped out to visit his aunt.'

Kit's mind chased after the train as fast as it could. He had to overtake it. Slowly, very slowly he gained upon it, first passing over the gold-laden wagon, then the train itself, and with a fresh burst of speed went racing on before it. He was tired and his magic at a low ebb, but he was determined to reach the station before Sparks and his crew.

He arrived and quickly sought out his aunt who gave a scream of surprise. *Come in—come in,* she cried. *Heavens, child, must you always zoom up in such a whirlwind? You gave me quite a scare—I thought that dreadful rat had returned.*

Listen, Aunt, said Kit. *Mr Sparks and his men are on their way to you. They have the gold and I reckon they also know about the secret passageway. It'll be the easiest thing in the world for them to take the gold up into your tower, specially now they've no guardian to fear.*

Why ever would they want to? asked Aunt Pearl.

Who knows? Perhaps to hide it there until there's less risk of being caught, but it means a lot of hard work so they will be too busy to care about you. Can you manage to creep out of the station and back down the line without anyone noticing? We're stuck in a cage, you see, and can't get out because Sparks has seen to it that the lock is well and truly magic-proofed.

Magic-proofed! snorted Aunt Pearl, and Kit felt her bosom rise like the figurehead on a man-of-war. *Why, nothing is magic-proofed as far as your Aunt Pearl is concerned.*

A few minutes later they heard the train pull into the station.

Take care, Aunt, said Kit bidding her goodbye.

With that, his mind raced back along the railway line; and when he opened his eyes he was startled to find his gang bending low over him, their faces a mixture of curiosity and anxiousness.

Seeing his eyelids flicker, May breathed out in relief. 'There,' she said, 'he's back home again, the lights have come on.'

Chapter Twelve

Not wanting to disturb his aunt in case he flustered her, Kit had no means of knowing what was going on at the next station—he, like the others, was forced to wait and hope for good news to arrive.

Then, after many nerve straining minutes, Aunt Pearl sent her mind to him. It gleefully reported that Sparks and his men were so preoccupied unloading their gold that she had slipped away as if nothing could be easier.

Now, nephew, she went on. *I will attempt to make my way by foot to you. I say 'attempt' since I daren't light a glow-ball to help me along, not yet anyway. Oh, this blessed dark tunnel is no place for a witch of my years. I keep wondering if I shall run into that nasty little rodent friend of yours . . .*

'What's happening?' demanded Fin when the look of concentration finally slipped from Kit's face.

Kit smiled and said simply, 'Aunt Pearl is on her way—she's coming to rescue us.'

'Hooray for Aunt Pearl!' shouted Alfie—she having been fully adopted by the whole gang by this time, indeed she appeared to have become 'Aunt Pearl' to everyone.

A loud cheer spread down the length of the cage with even Burrowers joining in; they whistled and clapped, despite having no idea why this person called *Ant Pool* was so important.

However, it didn't take long before the mood of excitement grew stale. Kit and his gang stood staring at the mouth of the railway tunnel waiting for the old woman to show; and when she didn't, boredom rapidly turned to impatience—and unwisely acting upon it Kit sent out his mind to find her. Fin, Alfie, Pixie, Gus, and even little Tommy followed him; and when they found Aunt Pearl they badgered and coaxed her along until she grew so heartily sick of them she swatted them away like a swarm of annoying gnats.

Stop pestering me! she said testily. **Or I shall trip over this bothersome railway line and do myself damage. Oh, if only I had my faithful broomstick to hand—if only!**

It was nearly half an hour later that Pixie finally spotted something.

'I can see a light!' she cried, suddenly leaping to her feet. 'Yes, look, there it is!'

Everyone squashed around her at the bars, eager to see. 'Aunt Pearl—here we are!' called Kit, waving his arms madly at her.

She appeared limping out of the tunnel, a picture of dejection, the flowers on her hat looking more wilted than ever. She had hitched up her dress and rolled down her stockings; and the glow-ball that now accompanied her was unkind enough to reveal a large smut on her nose.

She leaned against the tunnel mouth, panting heavily and sometimes blowing away loose strands of hair from her face, only to have them fall back down again, but she was too out of puff to fix them with magic.

'Quickly, Aunt, the door,' urged Kit.

'Hold your horses, boy,' she gasped. 'I'll be less than useless if I don't get my wind back first.' At last she stood up, straightened her hat and made her unsteady way up onto the platform, giving the lock a long, hard, purposeful stare as she approached it.

'It's a triple sure-shank,' explained Kit. 'We've all had a go at unpicking it, but none of us can.'

'It blunted my magic,' grumbled Gus.

'Huh,' scoffed Pixie, giving her brother a friendly dig with her elbow. 'Weren't that sharp to begin with.'

To Henry, May, and the other magic-less kids present, this talk of triple sure-shanks and blunted magic was way beyond their understanding. Likewise when they turned to the door of the cage they saw nothing more impressive here than a workaday padlock. It was all a complete mystery to them, for not having an enchanter's eyes they were unable to see the spell—a piece of cunning magic Bull Finnegan had cast in the form of a shining, complex knot, woven in and around the lock, protecting it and preventing it from being forced apart by another person's magic.

Aunt Pearl pushed back her sleeves. 'A challenge,' she said steely eyed. 'But I shall need help with this one, nephew.' And she ordered Kit to pull on one particular strand and Fin another and Gus yet a third. 'Stand in a semi-circle, that's it . . . give them room, everyone. Hush-hush, no talking there, please.' And when everything was to her liking she said, 'Right, nobody do a thing until I give the word, it's vital that we pull together and as hard as we can . . . Look to your magic now, wizards. Ready . . . steady—pull!'

Without anyone actually being anywhere near it, the cage door suddenly and violently rattled and the padlock jumped; and every time Aunt Pearl pointed it jumped again. Kit closed his eyes, this was proving more difficult than he'd imagined, it was proving more difficult than any of them had imagined: a battle of magic, just like in olden days when wizards jousted against each other to find who was the most powerful and cunning. Perhaps it was Bull after all. A stray spark of magic flew up from Fin and died with a crackle.

The others watched, gripped by fascination, some able to follow what was happening and some not. But to those who could it looked rather like a glowing snake was under attack and its only defence was to roll itself up into a tight ball; and whenever its head or tail was pulled free, it thrust it back into the middle of itself once more, becoming even more complex.

'All wizards and witches—hands on!' cried Aunt Pearl at her most commanding.

Pixie, Alfie, and Tommy joined in, pulling and pulling and pulling until there was an almighty flash which made all the Burrowers cry out in alarm and rush to the back of the cage.

Slowly the dense smoke cleared.

'Look—the door,' cried Tommy. 'It's open!'

And so it was. Without the need to be told, everyone poured out, making such a noise; and the Burrowers mobbed Aunt Pearl as if she were some kind of queen.

'Oh, really, you're far too kind,' she said hanging onto her hat.

'Come on,' called Kit. 'The battle hasn't prop'ly started yet, Sparks needs to be shown he can't go pushing us small people round no more.'

Everyone was for following him down the tunnel to the next station, but Aunt Pearl let out a cry of anguish. 'What? Walk all the way back—but I've only just arrived.'

'Perhaps you ought to stay here and rest if you're so tired,' suggested Henry respectfully.

Aunt Pearl looked scornful. '*Stay here?* I am not letting my no-good nephew out of my sight ever again—so you'd better think of something else, young man, and fast.'

In the end it was Aunt Pearl's devoted Burrowers who came up with the perfect solution. They quickly got a chair from the station, attached poles to it and indicated that if she sat upon it they would willingly carry her.

'In that?' said Aunt Pearl suspiciously.

'Hurry up, Aunt,' pleaded Kit. 'We need to catch up with ol' Sparks and his gang while we still have the chance.'

'Oh . . . very well, I suppose.'

Aunt Pearl, her expression full of silent suffering, sat on the chair. She gave a little gasp as the Burrowers lifted her shoulder high, before deciding she quite liked the idea of being carried by a horde of willing little men.

'Forward!' she cried dramatically. 'May magic win the day.'

As a small, excited army they entered the railway tunnel, Tommy and Alfie adding fire-crackers to their glow-balls—that was until Aunt Pearl complained that the noise gave her a dreadful headache and stopped them. Yet Kit worried that they still made too much noise.

'Quiet!' he ordered. 'Do you want Sparks and his bullies to hear us coming and be watching for us down the barrels of their rifles?'

They certainly did not. So with much less clamour than before they went on until at the far end of the tunnel they saw lights; and they immediately snuffed out their glow-balls in case they too were spotted.

The distant lights shone even brighter through the darkness. These were the gas lamps of St Paul's Underground station—as well as the red tail lamp of the getaway train pulled up at the platform.

'What do we do now?' asked Henry.

Kit shifted uncomfortably. The truth was he had no real idea, just a vague notion of using magic to make Sparks's life as difficult as possible. But Sparks's men had weapons. They would certainly fight back. No matter what, it was going to be dangerous. 'Let's check the lie of the land first, eh?' he said.

'Good idea,' said Henry enthusiastically, much to Kit's surprise.

With barely a murmur they crept the last few hundred feet along the tracks until the tunnel opened out into the station. The train hissed eerily but no one was in sight.

Touching Kit's shoulder, Fin pointed. 'The gold's been unloaded already,' he whispered. 'See, the gates are down on the wagon. It means they've only gone and got away with it, Kit.'

'That's impossible,' said Henry. 'All the exits are blocked, they must have been blocked again after Kit broke through them the last time. The gang has to be here somewhere.'

'Not necessarily,' said Kit. 'They went to a great deal of trouble to get Aunt Pearl out of the way. If they've taken the secret passageway they'd be up in the cathedral by now.'

'Then we have to go after them,' said Henry.

'No!' Kit stopped him. 'There's too many of us, we'll only get in each other's way; in any case we must get help and the quicker the better.' He grew thoughtful. 'The train maybe. Yes, if one of the Burrowers can drive it, then all those who don't have magic can head to the next working station and raise the alarm; while those of us who do have magic can set off after Sparks—if nothing else at least we can delay him.'

'Well, don't think you're leaving me behind,' said Henry firmly.

'Me neither,' said May. 'Someone has to keep an eye on Tommy.'

'Aw, May,' wailed Tommy. 'I can look after myself.'

'Tommy's right,' agreed Kit. 'We all can—we have our magic for protection. So if you two are coming along you must promise to stay at the back and shield yourselves behind one of us the moment we meet trouble.'

May and Henry both swore they would.

Then they set about getting everyone else aboard the

train. It was a tight squeeze, but finally Fin and Alfie shut and bolted the side gate.

'Be sure to give old Sparks a prickly spell down his trousers from us too,' shouted someone as the train puffed away.

Kit waved them goodbye, watching the red tail light disappear into darkness; and he and the group that remained on the platform moved closer together, suddenly feeling both few in number and that there was much for them to do.

'Come on,' said Kit turning and striding off. 'I'll show you where the secret passageway begins.'

'Not more gloomy tunnels,' groaned Pixie.

''Fraid so—here it is.'

Yet as he was about to start up it, Kit found himself skilfully elbowed aside by Aunt Pearl.

'Stay close behind me, nephew,' she instructed, taking the lead—and one glow-ball later the eight youngsters trooped in after her, Henry and May coming at the back as they'd promised. And, as they went along, Kit could hear his aunt crackle with magic, ready to shoot a lightning bolt at the first shadow to startle her, let alone any of Sparks's gang. But then Kit didn't expect to meet Sparks or his gang here, and he was right; and so without anything more threatening than spiders to deal with they emerged into the crypt.

'Coo, what a creepy old place full of creepy old things,' said Gus, gazing about with big, bug eyes.

If possible Tommy's eyes were even wider.

'Look, skeletons!' he uttered, slapping a hand to his mouth and the shriek that almost escaped it. 'Poor devils, did old Sparks do 'em in? Was he the one that topped 'em, eh, Kit?'

Kit smiled. 'Not very likely, Tommy,' he said. 'See, we're right underneath St Paul's so I 'spect some of these skulls and bones have lain here for hundreds of years. Most are older than your granny.'

'So it ain't Sparks's doing then?'

'No, Tommy.'

'Well I'm still not keen on how they keep on staring at me, like they're all reckoning mine's the next pile of bones to join 'em.'

Alfie being Alfie couldn't resist picking up the nearest skull, holding it before him like a mask and making a ghostly moan.

Tommy buried his face in May's chest, too frightened to look; while Aunt Pearl proved even less amused.

'That head does not belong to you, young man,' she said crisply. 'Remove it at once.'

And Alfie sheepishly did so, the skull this time appearing to grin at *him*.

Picking out a path through damp, mouldering tombs, they reached the stairs and went up them into the cathedral proper. Fin respectfully removed his pork-pie hat and clutched it to his chest; and Aunt Pearl snuffed out her glow-ball as a precaution, although an unnecessary one. Sparks had passed this way and gone. The cathedral was in almost complete darkness, just two candles burning distantly on the high altar. And despite its many stone pillars and buttresses, the ancient building seemed to hover over them as if the night air had been carved into arches, walls, and vaults; and for such a vast space it was so perfectly still and silent that Tommy's collar gradually crept up towards his ears in simple hair-prickling awe.

'Tread carefully over the floor,' warned Kit in the smallest of whispers. 'The slightest sound can echo badly in this place.' He was remembering the curmudgeonly bishop whose feet clip-clapped as he walked.

'Perhaps we ought to take off our boots altogether,' suggested Henry; and the twins agreed because their father had hammered big nails into the heels of theirs to prevent them from wearing out too quickly.

It was as they were untying laces and slipping off their boots that a strange sound was heard. At first they paid it no attention, but the persistent whirring grew steadily and impressively louder.

'That blimp's flying low,' said Gus glancing up, as if half expecting it to come crashing through the roof.

'Nah, that's not no blimp,' said Fin. 'Too many engines—must be one of the bigger airships.'

Henry stared across at Kit, now frantically ramming his feet back into his boots.

'Whatever's the matter?' he asked.

'The tower,' cried Kit, sprinting away and not caring how much noise he made. 'I think I know why Sparks needs it so badly!'

The others quickly pulled their boots back on too then followed him; Aunt Pearl hissing angrily that she would be left behind—until May and Pixie each caught an arm and half dragged her along with them.

'Thank you, my dears,' she gasped.

They caught up with Kit at the door leading to the tower stairs.

'It's locked on the other side,' he said darkly. 'I'm going to have to magic it open.'

The others looked extremely doubtful. Gus said, 'That won't do us no favours, Kit, Sparks is bound to hear you.'

'I doubt it,' replied Kit confidently. 'Besides, what can be heard above this?'

He gestured about him meaning the noise of the airship which had grown many times louder, and in the emptiness of the cathedral become an irritating drone that echoed from wall to wall, causing cascades of fine stone dust to come tumbling down like powdery waterfalls.

Aunt Pearl was outraged. She had to raise her voice to be heard. 'If it isn't enough in one night that villains have robbed the Bank of England, but we have hooligans trying to reduce the cathedral to a heap of rubble too—'

An explosive flash startled her into silence. The lock smoked and the door came creaking open to meet them. Before she could stop him, Kit slipped around it and vanished up the stairs. Determinedly Aunt Pearl barged her way forward and made sure she was next, but in doing so only managed to slow down the others who had no choice but to follow on behind.

Up and up the steep stairs Kit bounded; soon he was gasping for breath and his heart felt squeezed in his chest, and still the stairway kept on unwinding before him; while the ever present rumble of the airship's engines caused the darkness around him to throb.

He reached the broad landing where, beneath their coating of cobwebs, the cathedral bells had begun to vibrate—each bell sounding a single tremulous note. Mad with panic, bats swooped out of the darkness. Kit never broke stride. Coat tail flying he dashed to the next section of stairs and began to climb.

'Must be nearly there,' he croaked, his ears starting to hurt from the noise.

Stumbling, his outstretched hand struck a door. Kit fizzled with magic but it wasn't necessary—the door was unbolted. He turned a metal ring and gave a hard push. The door flew open. Immediately brilliant white light flooded in, along with a blast of wind created by twelve mammoth propellers—a man-made hurricane that swept away Aunt Pearl's crows like black rags and knocked Kit flat against the wall.

Recovering quickly he saw it was as he expected. The tower—the tallest building by far for miles around—was being used by Sparks to dock an airship. This was why time was so precious, the gang and gold had to rendezvous with it or everything was lost.

Kit squinted up his eyes to see better; with effort he noticed that the beam of bright light came from a searchlight on the airship's underside and, as his eyes grew more used to the harsh glare, he came to make out the form of the airship more clearly. It was black and sinister and tilted through the clouds at an angle; and there was not a single marking on it unless you included a crude skull and crossbones boldly painted on a tail fin. A crane was slowly winching up the gold on its port side, while on its starboard side the last of the gang followed each other up a rope ladder to the control room underneath. The overall sense was of ordered urgency; after all, most of London must have heard the airship's arrival, if not watching it in bewilderment at this very moment.

Dashing out onto the tower's deserted roof, Kit cupped his hands to his mouth and bellowed as loudly as he could above the engines' roar.

'Balthasar! Balthasar!'

The down-draught made him stagger as if caught in a tempest and his hair whipped wildly over his face.

'Balthasar! Balthasar!'

But it was no use. Even if Balthasar heard him he would not come, and why should he? Kit was not his master to command.

With tears pricking at his eyes, Kit searched around in wild desperation; inside him every just bone was aching to cheat Stafford Sparks of such an easy victory—whatever the cost; and in the next unthinking moment he flew across to the rope ladder and began to scramble up it.

He was in a kind of mad rage which did not leave him until he was halfway up and then for the first time saw ten thousand twinkling lights spreading away into the far distance. His stomach lurched. Too late he realized his mistake.

Worse soon followed.

For now the last of Sparks's gang had glanced down and spotted him. 'Where you been?' he shouted, mistaking Kit for one of his number. 'Get a shift on—we'll be shoving off out of here soon as the gold's aboard.'

But Kit did not move. He couldn't. He was too afraid. Above him the gold was swung through a set of double doors into the hold and the doors were slammed shut and secured behind it. Then the searchlight went out.

'Come on!' shouted the man, climbing the last few rungs into the control room. The mooring rope was unhitched and dropped heavily past Kit; and the instant it did he heard a charge in the engines, the steady rumble speeding up to a straining roar. The airship was moving— rising—even with his eyes shut tight Kit's stomach told him that; and at the same time he was set swinging—the rope ladder creaking under him as he flew in and out of the shadow of the monstrous black craft.

Never had Kit been more petrified than at that moment, his one clear thought being that the grip of his fingers was all that prevented him from falling to his certain death; yet the more this thought filled his head, the more slippery and numb his fingers became. Eyes closed he sensed the giddy sway through his body, almost as if he was fainting away. Suddenly he felt a need to be violently sick.

'Kit! Kit!'

Half heard below him he caught Henry's urgent shout. Then his voice was gone. Kit followed the black airship into dense, dark cloud.

'Grab him, lads, get him aboard.'

A new voice spoke, this time from above, and was not raised in a straining shout like Henry's, but speaking quite normally, albeit in a gruff unfriendly tone.

Kit forced himself to open his eyes and blinked away the wind-blown tears. The ladder with him still pressed to it was being winched into the airship. It gave Kit the horrible feeling of a great black spider reeling him in on the end of a thread. Hands reached down, seized him and pulled him through a trapdoor into the dimly lit control room.

Kit's glance fell upon brass tubes and blue glowing gauges and a large wooden wheel. Behind the wheel, steering the airship, was a uniformed captain, although all identifying badges of office had been removed from his cap and jacket, leaving little discoloured patches where they had been and a few loose threads hanging down.

Once Kit was safely aboard, the trapdoor was closed muffling the roar of the engines, but not their vibrations which Kit felt through his feet. As yet he still did not know whether to cry or be sick, but when he saw Stafford Sparks his will to do neither proved strongest. He glared angrily as Sparks advanced on him with a dirty rag.

'Well now, let's see who our brave little stowaway is,' he said. He spat on the rag and despite Kit's attempts to struggle, scraped it back and forth over his face until most of the grime was removed and his skin felt raw.

Sparks stepped back in surprise. 'Why, I know you,' he said. 'You're that . . . that witch doctor's wildcat son . . . Tell me what kind of game you think you're playing at here, boy? Eh? A dangerous one, believe you me—I ought to have you thrown overboard, back to the gutter where you and your type belong. Would you like that, boy? We'd soon see then if your mumbo-jumbo magic could do anything to save that grubby little neck of yours.' He gave a nasty laugh.

'The kid's a wizard?' said Bates warily. 'We can't afford to take no chances with a wizard aboard, boss.'

'Nor shall we, Bates,' said Sparks. 'Or can it be you're simply superstitious about a small, unwashed brat with a few cheap fizz-bangs up his sleeve? Look, you have rifles, man, beautifully machine tooled and oiled, the latest and most advanced of their kind. Science you see, Bates, it will win over everything in the end—including *witchcraft*.'

'What you going to do with me?' demanded Kit, surly with defiance.

Sparks toyed with the little silver spanner on his cravat and spoke teasingly. 'A problem that. Not so much mine, I feel, as yours. I still need to give it a little more . . . thought.' He smiled. 'I haven't completely decided against throwing you overboard yet, however much that may please me, so you'd better not think about trying to pull anything from your little box of magic tricks, because if you do . . . because if you do you may finally *persuade* me on the matter.'

'See, this is a pirate airship,' grinned Bates. 'And little boys we don't like are made to walk the plank.'

Kit glowered savagely at him but despite his brave words and looks, underneath he was frightened and his fear had shrunk his magic into a cold flame deep inside him.

Sparks turned away and peered at an altogauge. He waved his hand dismissively.

As Bates and two other armed men led Kit away, he wondered what his aunt and friends were doing. They were his last hope. Surely they wouldn't abandon him and do nothing at all?

Chapter Thirteen

Of course Kit was right. However, by the time his friends had jostled Aunt Pearl to the top of the stairway and spilt out onto the tower roof, Kit was no more than a distant figure rising rapidly into the night.

'What *is* that crazy child playing at?' said Aunt Pearl astonished.

Henry took several steps forward. 'Kit! Kit!' he shouted, his voice straining to be heard above the engines.

But Kit had disappeared into thick cloud and the sound of the airship had already begun to fade.

'Was there ever a boy born more rash?' declared Aunt Pearl, adding, 'Now give me room, dears, it is high time I started putting this nonsense to rights.'

And before their eyes she seemed to go through a change: no longer was she the batty old woman in a ridiculous hat, but a figure who commanded their respect and awe—a witch and guardian of ancient and very special powers. Slowly she raised her hands and closed her eyes.

'Gargoyles!'

Her call was immediately answered by the flap of unseen wings and an angry hiss.

The three men bundled Kit into the hold where the first thing he noticed was the gold bullion stacked up like common bricks in a builder's yard and secured with chains to stop it shifting in flight. In Kit's eyes it had become dull and uninteresting, but the men acted as if bewitched by it. They kept wandering over to it as if they couldn't believe such a prize was theirs; and when looking was not enough they touched and stroked it in an effort to convince themselves it was real. Bates even pulled out his handkerchief and spent time polishing it and making it shine; why the gold might have been his real reason for being there for all he cared about Kit, who was left half forgotten in a corner. Carelessly the men stood around bragging how they were going to squander their share of the fortune when they reached—

'Shhh,' said Bates suddenly. 'We said enough in front of the kid. Best we don't say no more.'

The other two remembered Kit's presence and scowled across at him as if he were responsible for ruining their pleasure. Grumbling they came back and sat on boxes around him, their rifles leaning against their legs or across their laps, yet Kit could tell their gazes and thoughts were still going back towards the gold.

His eyes searched about him: the hold was large but had been thoroughly cleared out to make as much room as possible for the precious cargo. The one external wall was reinforced with metal girders, cast with holes in them to reduce weight. Upon this wall was fixed a speaking-tube and a rack of glass fire grenades (like a row of little Christmas puddings), above which a sign began worryingly, 'In case of lightning strikes . . . ' Also along this wall were four portholes spaced evenly apart and the double loading doors.

Kit's gaze returned to the nearest porthole. The airship was passing through patchy cloud (probably to avoid detection) but, if he waited, there came longish moments of clear sky, during which he was able to see in detail two of the airship's twelve engines, their propellers spinning like silver discs.

Then with a jolt he glimpsed something else out there too and before he could stop himself he let out a gasp.

Luckily, at precisely the same moment the airship hit turbulence; it juddered and the support wires made a dull twanging sound. The men swayed against each other and put up their hands against the sides for balance. The turbulence lasted no more than seconds before the airship continued as smoothly as before—and no one bothered to remember Kit's burst of surprise.

Keenly now and with hardly a blink, Kit stared through the same porthole. Cloud went by like milky water, preventing him from seeing beyond a few feet. Then into a clear patch dotted with watery stars—and yes, something else besides stars, something which Kit was beginning to fear he had previously imagined. Seeing it truly real, he felt an uncontrollable leap of joy inside, and his cold flame of magic spread into a warming fire throughout his veins.

It was Balthasar!

Stretched long and lean in his efforts to keep up, the gargoyle's bat-like wings beat steadily against his body. As Kit watched, he drew up alongside the porthole and gazed in, his beautiful eyes meeting Kit's and holding them so powerfully that when Balthasar suddenly dipped and disappeared from view, Kit experienced a kind of emptiness that made him want to weep.

But Balthasar had disappeared for good reason.

A loud thud sounded against the outer doors.

Hearing it, one of the men snatched up his gun, his finger to the trigger.

'Take no notice—only more turbulence—' began Bates, when the doors came crashing inward—clawed and dented. In the opening, Balthasar announced his arrival with a low purring growl.

Only Kit was not thrown into total panic by this, his dramatic arrival. Of the three men, the first immediately turned and fled, shrieking as if his nightmares had broken through into the real world. The second raised his rifle, saying grimly, 'Whatever that *thing* is, I'm going to blast it—' But Bates grabbed the gun away.

'Are you completely off your head?' he yelled. 'It's a gargoyle! Bullets'll just ricochet off it, you might end up killing the both of us. Let's get Sparks—Sparks'll sort this out.'

Balthasar opened his mouth wide in a fine snarling display of fangs; and as he watched closely, Bates and his crony proceeded to edge nervously along the wall to the inner door. Then they bolted through it as fast as they could and went careering along the gangway to the control room, shouting out for Sparks like frightened little children calling for their mother.

Kit flew forward and gave the gargoyle a well deserved hug. 'Balthasar—oh, you were brilliant. A hero! Let me tickle your ears, you wonderful creature, you.'

Balthasar tilted his head as if giving his permission; he grinned dragonishly, his tongue hanging out between his bottom two fangs. Kit might have been content to stay there a good deal longer making a big fuss of him, had he not then heard Sparks come storming towards the hold.

'*What?* You mean to tell me you ran off and left the boy alone with the gold?'

'But what else could we do, boss?' protested Bates feebly.

Kit sidled up to the door and peered through its little round window. Sparks was advancing down the swaying gangway at the head of a large group of men, which bristled with rifles.

'This time he looks mad enough to throw me out of the airship and have done with it,' murmured Kit to himself. 'Hey, Balthasar—what d'you think you're doing?'

For just then Balthasar had flown up, softly sunk his fangs into Kit's collar, and was lifting him up so that only the toes of his boots touched the floor. At first Kit wanted to laugh out loud, feeling ridiculously like a kitten being lifted to safety by its mother-cat. But then, when he realized Balthasar meant to steer him towards the forced doors, then out of the airship altogether, he grew so alarmed he squirmed and struck out with his arms.

'No, Balthasar. Please no! It's too dangerous.'

The wind from the propellers blew keenly through the opening as they neared it, and what remained of the double doors groaned and creaked ready to fly off their hinges. Kit's feet left the floor and straightaway were snatched from under him by the icy pull of black air. He begged all the more to be set down, but Balthasar's jaw locked with a click, and he fought his way against the strong invisible current, wings straining to overcome it.

Sparks and his men burst in. They stared in disbelief at the gargoyle with the yelping boy in its jaws—like a lamb in the beak of an eagle.

'Shoot it! Shoot it!' raved Sparks. 'Aim for the wings and bring it down.'

By the time the first bullets sparked on jagged metal, Balthasar and Kit had gone.

Caught up in churning air, Kit was buffeted senseless—even so there was one thing that still managed to consume him and with a constant, blood-boiling passion—hatred of Balthasar; and as he grabbed blindly at the empty space before him, he was aware that with his every movement the stitching on his collar came a little more undone—giving way in a series of sickening little jerks. Soon, however, the airship had rumbled on its way, the many rows of portholes shining brightly in the darkness; and Kit was left to watch it go, hanging perfectly still now from the gargoyle's mouth.

'I . . . I'm sorry, Balthasar,' he whispered, realizing that in all probability Balthasar had saved his life.

No sooner had he spoken than there came a rush of air . . . and another . . . and another . . . each one a gentle breeze following the hurricane might of the airship's propellers, but they startled Kit all the same, until he saw Xerxes, Juno, and Philemon playfully swooping by to say their hellos. They were not alone—the remaining four gargoyles were also on the wing; and where there are gargoyles, the gargoyle-keeper is bound to be close by. Sure enough—

'Yoo-hoo—nephew!'

Aunt Pearl appeared riding her broomstick side-saddle in her usual elegant fashion; and Fin and Henry on Carpet shouted madly as they came racing up from below at what seemed a hundred miles an hour.

And not a minute too soon, for just then Kit's collar ripped clean off his jacket and he dropped neatly between his two friends, who made an urgent grab at him to stop him from rolling over the edge.

Kit sat up laughing.

'You see, the boy is plainly mad,' said Aunt Pearl fondly as she pulled up alongside. 'I can see absolutely no hope for the child.'

'None at all,' agreed Henry.

Suddenly Kit stopped laughing. 'But what about the airship?' he cried. 'Sparks and his gang are getting away.'

'Oh, let them enjoy their moment's victory,' said Aunt Pearl. Unhurriedly she summoned her gargoyles to her, calling each one by name. In answer they dived down and flew above her head, snout-to-tail in a tight circle.

'Listen and listen well,' Aunt Pearl told them seriously. 'You have been patient and waited long enough, but now is the time for you to do your work. Time for claws and time for fangs. You know what has to be done, see to it that no gargoyle does any more or any less—now *go*, and good hunting to all eight of you.'

When she finished speaking, Gotheric suddenly broke free of the circle and the others flew after him in a line. They flew fast and purposefully, with ears back and heads down as though diving from a great height; Aunt Pearl's broomstick and Carpet scarcely kept pace.

Slowly the black airship came back into sight, although by this time the gargoyles had flown so far ahead they were only visible whenever they crossed in front of its lights. Reaching their quarry, they immediately broke rank and began to mob the craft like small birds attacking a far bigger one—but Sparks was ready for them. Kit heard gunshot, and a haze of blue gun smoke quickly formed at half a dozen portholes.

'They best watch out for themselves,' murmured Fin worriedly, for from a distance it sounded like a regular battle, but one very much in Sparks's favour.

'Don't worry,' said Kit 'Look—'

They saw that the rattle of guns acted as no more than a signal to the gargoyles, telling them to stop their play and set about the attack in earnest. Balthasar led it, diving down with spread claws to the fore like a fistful of scalpels. Without pausing he caught the flank of the airship and a small gash appeared in its taut skin. The other gargoyles did exactly the same at different points all around.

The airship's flight became affected at once, it started to list like a dying fish; and one by one the engines spluttered to a standstill. The airship was sinking, slowly at first then more and more quickly as it lost gas and buoyancy.

Suddenly a white streak lit up the night.

'Watch out, they're firing magic at us!' shouted Fin, but Henry shook his head.

'It's a distress flare,' he said sadly; for it did make a sad sight, the once mighty airship slipping between clouds that towered over it like icebergs.

Aunt Pearl was thinking ahead. 'Come on,' she cried. 'And have your best magic and wits about you—it will be dreadful if anyone gets hurt unnecessarily, especially if it lies in our power to prevent it.'

With a kick of her heels against her broom she went spiralling down alongside the stricken airship; Kit ordered Carpet to keep up. Below them lay London stretched out in all directions, its streets and houses close together, and the airship coming down on them like a storm cloud.

'Over there, look!' said Henry pointing. 'That must be Hyde Park. What do you think? I'd say that's as good a place to land an airship as any.'

Kit followed his finger and saw a large patch of darkness surrounded by twinkling city lights.

'Perfect,' he agreed, sounding much relieved. 'And if Fin helps me to raise a lively wind charm it'll put down there for sure.'

'Careful, nephew,' warned Aunt Pearl. 'Don't overshoot the mark.'

'Don't worry, Aunt,' said Kit beginning his magic.

A wind charm as any wizard will tell you is a simple piece of magic—simple and effective in this case. Without engines, the airship proved as easy to manoeuvre as a child's balloon. Fin and Kit guided it over the centre of the park with hardly a moment to spare: dark trees and dim paths were fast looming up to meet it, as well as a line of electricity pylons that stood proud of even the park's tallest trees, like a row of spying giants. The pylons were cast iron and had been designed by Stafford

Sparks himself, who meant them to resemble the type of columns found on ancient temples (yet somehow they still managed to be extraordinarily ugly). Kit saw a collision with them was unavoidable—no magic could help now—and he watched helplessly, waiting for events to play themselves out.

Moments later there came a horrible grating of metal and the smash of glass, followed by a tremendous flash and wild scattering of sparks. The night crackled with blue light as cables broke free and fell to the ground, thrashing about there like living things.

With cables and pylons felled, much of the heart of London—including Buckingham Palace—went dark, but the darkness was not so complete it hid the fate of the airship. As in slow motion Kit saw it roll further onto its side.

'It's heading straight into the Serpentine Lake,' he cried.

In its last dying seconds the airship struck water leaving a white scar of foam in its wake. Then the lake seemed to catch it—pull it down. The airship dropped heavily, breaking the lake's smooth face into a confusion of towering waves. Metal crumpled upon metal, and went on doing so for what seemed minutes until at last the airship lay still, the skull and crossbones fin rising like a sail above the heaving water that smashed against it. This apart, the airship was quite unrecognizable, its smooth, rounded body now burst into an ugly tangle of twisted girders and wires, like ribs thrusting through skin.

Presently, out of doors and holes and escape hatches, men were seen to clamber, some pulling themselves higher to safety, others diving straight into the cold, black water and swimming for land. The last few cabin lights left working flickered several times then went out for good; and through the silence Kit heard the clanging bells of police vans steaming full pelt to the scene.

'Oh dear,' said Aunt Pearl tragically. 'I hope we haven't caused too great an inconvenience.'

Chapter Fourteen

The next morning London awoke to rumours so outrageous that the biggest liar in the world would blush to repeat them. Soon, outside every newspaper office in Fleet Street crowds began to gather, mostly made up of people unable to believe a single word of these rumours true unless they saw it in bold print; and the moment any unsuspecting paperboy poked his nose through a door the crowds were upon him, losing their hats and dignity in the scramble, snatching newspapers from beneath his arm and fighting amongst themselves for the latest scoop.

Bank of England ROBBED! shouted one headline.

Airship crashes in central London, bellowed another, adding in thankful relief, *No serious injuries reported*.

Yet a third yelled, *Queen's close adviser arrested*.

Tucked away in some editions, but not all, was a whisper about a gang of juvenile wizards and witches who had been arrested in Hyde Park under suspicion of being somehow involved in the robbery. Their leader, went on these reports, was an elderly witch in a flowered hat. All those placed under arrest were being held at the Tower of London until further notice.

Kit sat on a hard wooden bench, staring up at a high barred window, his head in his hands and his elbows on his knees. Despite the bucket of ice cold water in the corner, he was only slightly cleaner than before; and he was dressed in an arrowed prison uniform many sizes too large for him, with the cuffs and the trousers rolled up. The uniform smelt disgusting—as if it hadn't been washed from the previous prisoner who had worn it, while across the back for the whole world to see, was printed in large black letters, PROPERTY OF H.M. PRISONS.

Kit sighed. This was not how he expected his adventures to end, arrested by a wizard detective and snapped into a pair of magic-proof handcuffs. They all had been, even Aunt Pearl who kept moaning about the disgrace of it and scanning the crowds that arrived on the scene at the same time as the police, to see if she recognized anyone there who might, heaven forbid, spread word of her 'brush with the law' to her respectable circle of witch friends. Then a police steam van was brought in to carry them off to the Tower; and despite his loud protests Kit had been placed in a cell all by himself, his magic within him a pale shadowy flicker; yet had it not been, had it been raging like a furnace instead, the thick iron door before him would have soundly defeated it. He sighed again and watched a beam of frosty sunlight move slowly up the wall opposite—outside a lone werewolf bayed.

Then he supposed he must have fallen into a doze, sitting upright on the edge of the bench. The next thing he knew was a key rattling in the lock, then a yeoman guard in his red, black, and gold uniform entered; he carried a pike, the sort of thing Kit imagined was used in the olden days to chop off wrongdoers' heads . . .

'The prisoner will stand,' he said coldly.

Kit slipped off the bench, but even when standing he felt very small and insignificant before his broad, bearded jailer.

'You have a visitor, Prisoner Stixby,' said the yeoman, and he stepped aside, left the cell and the heavy door boomed closed.

As soon as Kit glimpsed his father's emerald-green top hat, his eyes brimmed with tears. He fell back onto the bench, full of shame and remorse, and with his face pressed to his hands he wept until he shook; and with his tears flowed broken snatches of his story. He wasn't a criminal—he wasn't, he said over and over again. And if Mr Sparks claimed he was, then he was a big fat bare-faced liar!

'I know, Kit, I know,' said his father soothingly; and removing his hat he sat quietly waiting beside him. Eventually Kit could cry no more and the moment he stopped he realized that his father had placed his arm around him. Now, it was a curious thing but having it there made Kit feel so much better, despite his seemingly endless troubles; and his magic responded inside him, perking up and making him a little more like his old self.

'Now, come along,' said Dr Stixby. 'I should like you to come with me.'

Kit stared at him, his nose and eyes very red. 'What . . . leave the Tower, you mean?' he said in disbelief.

'That much has been arranged,' answered Dr Stixby. He held out Kit's collar-less jacket to him, as much to hide his prison rags as to keep him warm, then crossed to the door; the yeoman outside opened it, once it had been banged upon for him to do so.

At they stepped out, the yeoman nodded his head towards Kit, saying not in an unkindly way to Dr Stixby, 'He needs a close eye keeping on him does that one.'

'Yes,' agreed Dr Stixby. 'I see that clearly at long last.'

The yeoman handed Kit his flying carpet, rolled up and struggling against the string that tied it. The yeoman used his penknife to cut it free and the instant he did, Carpet flung itself at Kit, wrapping around him like a loving boa constrictor.

Dr Stixby stood watching awkwardly.

'If you have no objections, Kit, I should like to travel on Carpet with you,' he said. 'I arrived by blimp this morning so it will be more convenient for me if we could share a ride together.'

Kit certainly didn't object, although he thought it rather odd, his father having never ever ridden on Carpet with him before, even in the days when he was very young and learning how to fly.

Wanting to create a good impression, Kit ordered Carpet to lie still ('play dead', he called it) and stop acting the brainless puppy. Dr Stixby climbed aboard, not knowing what to do with his long spindly legs or whether to sit or kneel.

'I'm rather more at home with a broom,' he confessed. 'So if you don't mind I'll hold on to you until I get the hang of it.' And with that he put both his hands around Kit's waist.

Again Kit didn't mind—indeed he felt his magic flicker warmly as if another log had been thrown to the flames. He turned his head. 'Where to now, Father? Home, I suppose.'

'Eh?—oh no, no,' said Dr Stixby absently. 'Buckingham Palace and without delay, if you please.'

'*Buckingham Palace?*' repeated Kit in surprise—and Carpet, believing this its order, rose so sharply that Kit was unable to ask why.

After a brief flight Carpet landed before the Palace. Kit gazed at the building's forbidding front.

'You sure us Stixbys are welcome here?' he asked doubtfully.

Dr Stixby rose brushing himself down. 'Well, Kit,' he said, 'the Queen *is* Henry's grandmother after all, and as such has a perfect right to hear for herself your side of events. Don't forget that in her eyes you're no better than a common kidnapper.'

'*What?* . . . I reckon I better go straight back to the Tower,' said Kit gloomily. 'Leastways it will save the Queen the bother of having to send me there afterwards.'

But already it was too late to think of going anywhere. Two footmen had arrived, one to direct them into the palace and one to carry Carpet, which was behaving particularly badly that morning, trying to flick off the footman's powdered wig. Kit struggled not to laugh, especially at the way the footman tried to pretend nothing was happening and carried on staring straight ahead. But then Kit remembered the deep trouble he was in and had little problem in keeping a straight face, indeed it grew positively grim.

Inside the palace a surprise awaited. After they had climbed some steps they came to one of the formal corridors, along which a number of workmen could be seen atop of ladders, unscrewing things from the walls, leaving grubby fingerprints behind on the old Chinese wallpaper and gilt picture frames (both footmen raised eyebrows in despair on noticing this). And where the workmen had been already, Kit saw tangles of wires hanging through holes.

'The Queen ordered it herself,' explained Dr Stixby hardly able to disguise his delight. 'After you—er, the airship, I mean—left the palace without a single light, she decided that electricity is simply too modern and unreliable. Therefore she has ordered the removal of everything electrical from the building, and Mr Horgan her old lighting wizard has been offered back his job.'

'Well, that's one in the eye for Mr Sparks,' said Kit with a nod of satisfaction.

'If I were you, Kit, I wouldn't mention the name of that particular person in front of her majesty,' said Dr Stixby, his voice falling to a whisper. 'It wasn't only electricity that the Queen took against last night. Ah, we're here—'

Kit swallowed nervously. They had halted in front of a set of tall double doors, each door with a magnificent golden coat of arms upon it. Before allowing the footmen to proceed, Dr Stixby made a hurried attempt at getting his son to look more presentable, wiping his face with a handkerchief and trying to flatten his wilful hair with a lick and a smooth of his hand.

'Aww—Dad—the footmen are staring at me,' said Kit embarrassed, but probably more delighted that his father should want to make such a fuss of him.

'Ahh . . . that will do, I suppose,' said Dr Stixby unconvinced. He cleared his throat, removed his emerald-green top hat and, after tucking it firmly beneath his arm, said, 'Lead on, my man—lead on.'

The double door swung open. A long room with mirrors down one side and views across the gardens to the lake and island, on the other, presented itself to Kit. He blinked against the brilliance of so many highly polished surfaces. Overhead, special glow-ball chandeliers glittered, and the thickness of the carpet made itself known even through the soles of Kit's battered boots. The carpet was purple and seemed to flow to the room's furthest end, where it trickled up six steps to a raised position and a throne.

Nor was this any old throne (if ever they are!). This particular one was a gift from the Nabob of Bengal. Its seat was tiger skin, and its arms tiger paws, and its back a huge fan of peacock feathers; it had no legs nor need of them because two large crane's wings on either side supported it off the ground, beating regularly but without the slightest sound or disturbance to the air. Of course it was nothing less than the work of the Nabob's wizards—a magic throne—and seeing the Queen's little figure seated upon it, Kit felt her approval of all things magical and grew extremely proud.

But then, catching the Queen looking at him, he was

reminded he was here on quite a different business. To be truthful he was unable to tell much from the royal expression: was she going to be cold and disdainful, or outright furious with him?—after all, hadn't Henry told him often enough that the Queen had a temper.

By her side was Mr Gladstone, her Prime Minister, who every few minutes bowed his head to whisper something in her ear, and each time the Queen waved him away irritably. At last she squeezed one of the tiger-paw arms and the throne growled, drawing everyone's attention wonderfully—as only a tiger growl could.

'Ah, witch doctor,' said the Queen. 'I see you have brought your son—the prisoner.'

'I have indeed, Ma'am,' replied Dr Stixby bowing gravely.

'Now, Mr Gladstone, be kind enough to read out how we mean to deal with him in the matter for which he stands accused.'

'But I haven't done nothing wrong!' wailed Kit. 'Not unless it's wrong to save the whole kingdom and . . . and prob'bly Henry's life into the bargain.'

'Hush, boy,' hissed his father. 'Speak only if spoken to, otherwise hold your tongue.'

Mr Gladstone peered over a lengthy document as if to ask, 'Are the interruptions over yet?', then in a dry, monotonous voice he began to read.

'It is hereby decreed by our most sovereign majesty, Victoria Regina, in the presence of her Privy Council and with full accord of said majesty's government—'

The Queen made her throne growl at him and he jumped with fright.

'For goodness' sake, Mr Gladstone,' she snapped, '*do* get on with it. No need to bother with the dry bits, skip to the interesting part . . . tell us the interesting part, man.'

'Yes, Mr Gladstone, please do,' said a voice from

behind the throne, and out strolled Henry, hands in pockets, as if by chance happening to pass that way. And before Kit had time to blink he was joined by Fin, Alfie (laughing like a hyena), the twins Gus and Pixie, Tommy and May; with Aunt Pearl coming last of all, sporting a new hat for the occasion—a mass of cascading daffodils.

'But . . . but . . . I don't understand,' stammered Kit.

Dr Stixby smiled and put his arm around Kit's shoulders. 'As you said yourself, son, you've done nothing wrong. Quite the opposite in fact; why, Kit, I don't think I could be any prouder of you if I tried.'

'Oh, my dreadful nephew,' cooed Aunt Pearl, affectionately chucking him under the chin. 'Such a terrible boy—his wickedness quite takes your breath away.'

And everyone burst out laughing, even Mr Gladstone managing a tight diplomatic smile. Then there arose an unmistakable hiss.

'Balthasar!' cried Kit as the gargoyle crawled out from beneath the flying throne. Kit threw himself at him, while Balthasar sat like a great cat, enjoying every scrap of affection.

'Dear old Balthasar,' said Kit burying his face into his scaly neck.

'Now there's a sight one does not see every day, Prime Minister,' commented the Queen peering hard at the gargoyle. 'Not even here at the Palace.'

Only much later did Kit finally discover how the Queen meant to reward him (not punish him as he first believed); and it appeared there was to be something for everyone else too. Dr Stixby became Sir Charles Stixby, receiving through the post a smart new emerald-green topper in time for the knighting ceremony; Aunt Pearl was given a pearl necklace and a medal, and had a style of hat named after her; and everyone—Burrowers and youngsters alike—who had been involved in either raising the alarm or the capture of Sparks's gang, was each given a hundred pounds (which was a lot of money in those days).

Furthermore, it was announced one morning in *The Times* that Kit, Tommy, Fin, Alfie, Pixie, and Gus were to be sent to Eton—the finest magic academy in the world—their fees and school gowns fully paid for them. They were due to start in the new year.

'Ain't it another school?' said Gus suspiciously when told the news. None of the gang liked school.

'I hear tell how la-di-da it is up there,' added Alfie. 'They have to wear these soppy gowns with big blue stars on 'em.'

'That should suit you, Alf,' said Pixie dodging a playful cuff.

It needed a lot of persuading on Kit's part before the gang accepted it was being sent to no ordinary place of learning.

'We'll be able to do advanced magic and stuff,' explained Kit. 'Not just ol' sums and pages of copying, but shape-shifting and invisibility. Can you think of anything better than spending all day doing nothing but magic?'

'And what about me?' demanded May.

That was a problem. May had no magic in her—yet it was eventually agreed she should go to Eton with the others but attend a nearby girls' school, a *posh* school as she never tired of telling anyone who'd listen: this left her plenty of time to do what she really enjoyed best—getting everyone else organized . . . sometimes better known as bossing.

As for Henry, he had other duties to perform. But in the long summer holidays everyone was allowed to visit him at Windsor Castle, where the gang and its outrageous tricks were looked forward to and dreaded in equal measure by all the servants.

However, that was way off into the future. For the present the stolen gold had to be recovered from the Serpentine, which it was by a floating crane, while armed Chitterbugs from the Royal Air Army hovered overhead.

Stafford Sparks had been captured at the scene of the crash, prevented from running away by a broken leg. Most of his gang had been captured in the park too, and the small number who escaped were not free for long. The police also arrested Bull Finnegan. He was discovered hiding in a coffin at a certain undertaker's, who was led away to prison with him, pelted with cabbages and rotten tomatoes by bands of jeering children.

For several days after Bull's arrest, Fin was so downhearted that nothing his friends did could cheer him up.

'I only got myself left to call family,' he told them sadly.

May took Kit aside. 'We ought to do something about this,' she said. 'Poor Fin, it's not right him moping around. He'll make himself ill if he ain't careful. What he needs is something to cheer him up, something to take him out of himself.'

An idea came to Kit like an arrow shot. 'Why not?' he said, agreeing with it aloud; then he was off calling for Carpet.

'Here, where you going?' demanded May, narrowing her eyes at him as if he were peculiar.

'Wait and find out,' shouted Kit. He rose into the air on Carpet; and looking down he rudely touched his nose making the 'nosy' sign at her.

'Oh, very nice,' said May folding her arms.

That night the gang met as usual on the gasometers by St Pancras station. It was a cold night and the stars were

163

out—a perfect night for playing soot bombs. But nobody felt like having any fun. It simply felt too disloyal to Fin, who sat a little apart sighing deeply from time to time.

'Where's Kit?' whispered Gus to his sister. 'Wish he would come. Boring here without him.'

Pixie shrugged. 'May told me he suddenly dashed off on Carpet, but she said he was definitely up to something.'

'Sounds like Kit,' chuckled Gus admiringly.

Something crossed before the face of the moon making them all look up—all that was except Fin.

'Kit!' cried Alfie, leaping to his feet and grabbing his broom in the hope they might be going somewhere.

But Kit landed and stepped off Carpet.

'I'd like you to meet a friend,' he said. 'In fact I 'spect he's going to join our gang.'

'Where?' asked Gus, making a big show of searching around. 'Invisible is he?'

'Told you he was acting a bit—' May twiddled a finger by the side of her head. Pixie nodded.

Kit went across to Fin, his hand slipping into his pocket. Fin looked up at last and saw that Kit was offering him something. Puzzled, Fin took it and was surprised to find it was soft, warm, and furry.

'The only name he answers to is Rat, I'm afraid,' said Kit, watching Fin pet the little creature. 'He's excellent at chewing through ropes—oh, and he's extremely fond of biscuits.'

Burrower villages are no longer marked on plans of the Underground, found, say, at the backs of diaries. Indeed, these days most villages are not on the main railway routes at all, so reaching them must once again be done through the ancient foot tunnels.

Other books by Stephen Elboz

A Land Without Magic
ISBN 0 19 271875 4

The second book in a series about Kit Stixby and his magical adventures.

'Stafford Sparks has escaped from prison!' Hearing that name again was like an icicle piercing Kit's stomach. He had wanted to forget all about that evil magic-hater and his mad ideas to control the world through science . . . Now this . . .

With the arch-criminal Stafford Sparks on the loose again, Kit and his friend Prince Henry could be in terrible danger. So Kit is sent to Paris, out of harm's way, and Prince Henry goes to Callalabasa for the king's coronation. But then Kit learns that Henry's bodyguard is one of the magic-haters and Henry is in even greater danger.

Kit rushes after his friend, determined to protect him, not realizing that in Callalabasa magic is forbidden and the slightest trace of enchantment is punishable by death. How can Kit look after Henry and defeat the evil plans of the magic-haters if he can't use his magic powers? And just why is Callalabasa so important to so many people? Just when all seems lost, help arrives from an unexpected quarter . . .

The Tower at Moonville
ISBN 0 19 275093 3

Moonville is a very strange school—there are no lessons and the boys are left to run riot. On the run from his wicked uncle, Nathan wonders what kind of mad world he has stumbled into.

He takes refuge in the tower with the mysterious scientist who lives there. But he can't hide away for ever and when his uncle finally catches up with him, Nathan finds himself in great danger . . .

Ghostlands
ISBN 0 19 275092 5

From the moment Ewan steps through the door of the house, he realizes that this will be no ordinary visit. For one thing, Ziggy lives there—and Ziggy's a ghost. And where there's one ghost, there are bound to be others . . .

Ziggy and his ghoulish friends are in terrible danger. The local ghost-nappers are out to trap them and are not above a spot of devious magic to get what they want. And what has the theme park, Ghostlands, got to do with all this . . . ?

A Store of Secrets

ISBN 0 19 275067 4

Bridie can't understand it. Has Gramps vanished into thin air? And what are the peculiar Crickbone twins doing in his yard?

All alone in the city, Bridie stumbles across the Byzantium Bazaar, a crumbling department store crammed with cats and cobwebs. And as she tries to discover the truth behind Gramps's mysterious disappearance, other deeply held secrets slowly begin to emerge . . .

The House of Rats

ISBN 0 19 275021 6

Winner of the Smarties Young Judges Prize

The great house has become a dangerous place since the master mysteriously vanished. Wolves prowl around in the snow outside, hungry and howling, while inside the house, the horrible Aphid Dunn has taken charge. Everything seems to be falling apart.

Esther and the boys are wondering if things can get any worse, when they discover a whole new world under the house. There might still be one last chance at freedom after all . . .

Temmi and the Flying Bears

ISBN 0 19 275015 1

Temmi is furious when the Witch-Queen's soldiers come to the village to steal one of the flying bears—even more so when he discovers that they've taken Cush, the youngest cub, who is Temmi's favourite bear. Temmi is determined to rescue Cush, but instead finds himself captured and taken to the Ice Castle where he will be a prisoner, too. Escape seems impossible— unless Temmi can somehow win over the ice-hearted Queen . . .